T0303594

PRAISE FOR *THE WOMEN'S COURTYARD*

'One of the iconic modern Urdu novels. Basically about the Partition—and about how people observed it in the prospect, and what actually happened to them—it is a highly symbolic narrative of fractured lives and peoples. Poignant, and in many ways somehow prophetic of the events that happened much later after Partition, it is a novel that deserves much greater notice than it has received so far. It is a good thing that Daisy Rockwell, a knowledgeable and committed translator from Urdu and Hindi, has chosen to bring this truly great novel—and not just by a woman, but great by any standards—novel before the wider world through her English translation.'
SHAMSUR RAHMAN FARUQI

'Beyond the astute, masterful exercise of a translator's art, her sensitive choices in diction and idiom, Daisy Rockwell's translations are rendered with a subtle brilliance that transports our master writers' original framework of sensibilities with great delicacy into a new language. We are fortunate to have, in Rockwell, a meticulous, virtuoso translator working on our literature.'
MUSHARRAF ALI FAROOQI

'[*The Women's Courtyard*] is at its core an indictment of patriarchy—one of the most moving and powerful in all our fiction . . . Mastur gives us a narrative on the epic scale, ranging across four generations, the life-arcs of dozens of characters—births, marriages, suicides, imprisonments, sexual assault, divorce—and taking in Gandhi's leadership of the national movement, the rise of the Muslim League, and the birth of Pakistan. The narrative is always gripping . . . Rockwell's translation is superbly judged. Her English renders the spareness of Mastur's Urdu, the efficiency of her physical descriptions, and the devastating concision with which she handles tragedy.'
KESHAVA GUHA, *THE HINDU*

'I picked up this 400-page novel and devoured it in two sittings. Powerful storylines fluently told in a deceptively simple and colloquial style, strong, outspoken characters and plenty of action kept the pages turning. Woe betide you if you skip a chapter— you will miss another key twist in the plot . . . Daisy Rockwell is

A
Promised
Land

experienced and highly accomplished and it's no surprise that her [translation] is such a joy . . . Mastur is an expert at indicating her characters' thoughts and feelings in a brief phrase, a description of a detail, often just in a gesture.'
GILLIAN WRIGHT, *OPEN*

'Khadija Mastur's classic novel *Aangan* receives a superb and nuanced new translation that is likely to garner even more admirers for the book . . . Rockwell's highly readable version makes me approach the novel with as much excitement as did reading it for the first time many years ago . . . Rockwell's version makes me want to rush back to the original and this is her real success as a translator.'
ASIF FARRUKHI, *DAWN*

'An unrelentingly bleak portrayal of poverty, deprivation and the needless cruelties of time and circumstance. However, there is plenty here for those interested in a nuanced reading of patriarchy . . . Daisy Rockwell's immaculate translation of Khadija Mastur's *Aangan* is welcome not only for bringing the work to English readers, but also as a feminist tract that questions love, marriage and the need for happy endings.'
RAKHSHANDA JALIL, *INDIA TODAY*

'The novel is as much an indictment of a patriarchal system as it is a comment on the fragmenting of nations. . . The continually shifting equation of the friction and solidarity between the women layers the novel with complexities—there are no easy character evaluations, no sure stances on the choice between India and Pakistan, or between wanting a liberated lifestyle and a secure family. Aliya, the focal character . . . asserts her own will . . . The pitfalls of marriage, the obscuring of sexual violence within the family, the muting of sexual agency, and the uncertainty of political movements, all play out through [Aliya's] observations of the world. The personal rings with the political in every way . . . The story doesn't fail to captivate, feigning the smallness of a domestic portrait while quietly writing the saga of a family, its women and its nations.'
POORNA SWAMI, *MINT*

A Promised Land

KHADIJA MASTUR

Translated from the Urdu by
DAISY ROCKWELL

PENGUIN BOOKS

An imprint of Penguin Random House

PENGUIN BOOKS

USA | Canada | UK | Ireland | Australia
New Zealand | India | South Africa | China | Singapore

Penguin Books is part of the Penguin Random House group of companies
whose addresses can be found at global.penguinrandomhouse.com

Published by Penguin Random House India Pvt. Ltd
4th Floor, Capital Tower 1, MG Road,
Gurugram 122 002, Haryana, India

First published in Penguin Books by Penguin Random House India 2019

ISBN 9780670090358

Typeset in Adobe Caslon Pro by Manipal Digital Systems, Manipal
Printed at Replika Press Pvt. Ltd, India

www.penguin.co.in

This is a legitimate digitally printed version of the book and therefore might not
have certain extra finishing on the cover.

Contents

Preface

A Promised Land was Khadija Mastur's second novel, first published four years after her death in 1987. Though it was not technically a sequel to her first novel, *The Women's Courtyard*, it begins at the same time period that the first one left off (1947, after the Partition of India and Pakistan), and in the same place—Lahore, at the Walton Camp, the refugee camp where Aliya, of *The Women's Courtyard*, was volunteering. This time, the protagonist, Sajidah, is a refugee living in the camp. She comes from more humble beginnings than Aliya (though Aliya was living in poverty before the Partition, hers had been an illustrious land-owning family), but otherwise the two share many similarities: each is smart, educated, independent in her thinking, but constrained by her gender and role in society. *A Promised Land* can thus be considered a sequel in terms of Mastur's philosophical trajectory, if not in the strict sense of a continued narrative thread.

While *The Women's Courtyard* was an exploration of women's roles within the family space delineated by the inner courtyard, or *aangan* (which is the original Urdu title), Mastur focuses on a feminist critique of the patriarchal underpinnings of territorialism and feudalism in *A Promised Land*. The original title of the novel is *Zameen*, another common two-syllable word (like aangan) that contains multitudes. Zameen means land, earth, property, territory, and is the essential unit of ownership in a feudal society—landowners are called *zamindar*s. Zameen also refers to the newly formed country—Pakistan—a new homeland, a promised land, for Muslims. Zameen is that little bit of earth that Sajidah and her father lived on in Delhi before the Partition, and the tiny 'home' they created with sheets and cots in the refugee camp.

A Promised Land is a much shorter book than *The Women's Courtyard*, but it has a powerful philosophical sweep. Here, Mastur takes on the promises made and broken within the state of Pakistan after its creation and offers a scathing feminist critique of the neo-feudalism that takes hold of the society post-Partition. What does the thirst for ownership of land and counting one's acres mean for women in this new country? How can the promise of Pakistan as a place of safety for all Indian Muslims maintain that egalitarian ideal in the face of greed for territory? And what provisions are there for the safety and independence of women in a patriarchal system that views women as possessions less valuable than parcels of land?

Daisy Rockwell

Translator's Note

Once upon a time, a translator into English would have had a clear idea of the location and reading needs of her readership. If one published a translation in New York, one wrote for the US market; in Delhi, it was for the Indian market. But nowadays, with the advent of global book distribution and electronic books, an English translation published in Delhi, or London, or Sydney, will instantly be available via various online resources anywhere in the world. This makes the readership very wide indeed, and though I strive to reach out to all potential readers, there will always be some for whom I have translated too much, and others for whom I've translated too little.

A prime example of this dynamic is in the vexed question of how to translate kinship terms. Readers of English in India and Pakistan that come from Hindi–Urdu-speaking backgrounds often retain all the Hindi and Urdu kinship terms in their English speech. These readers find it jarring to read words like *dadi* (paternal grandmother) rendered as 'granny', or *mausi* (maternal aunt) as simply 'aunt' or 'aunty'. For readers who know no Urdu or Hindi, however, trying to master the kinship terms can become an insurmountable obstacle to enjoyment, even if there is a glossary.

My solution has been to try to seek a compromise. I usually leave in some of the original terms, but I don't retain all. For example, one person's *phuphi* (paternal aunt) is another person's *bhabhi* (sister-in-law) is another person's *didi* or *apa* (elder sister) is another person's *poti* (granddaughter). This would mean learning four different vocabulary words for one person, and as is clear from the sentence, none of these words is untranslatable into English. My solution has been to retain some kinship terms but to avoid having most characters referred to by too many different Urdu terms. In *A Promised Land*, for example, I've retained the terms *Khala Bi* (aunt) and *Amma Bi* (mother) because these titles function as names in the text. In fact, it is a fortunate idiosyncrasy within the family that these titles are used by everyone, including Sajidah—the newcomer—who is related to neither of the two women. Another familial idiosyncrasy is that the head of the family is called Malik (master) by one and all, and never addressed as Abba (father) or any of the words that mean 'uncle'. Thus, his term of address is also non-relational.

When I do retain Urdu words in the translation, I try to make sure that their meaning is clear from context. If everyone is sitting around eating omelettes and *paratha*s for breakfast, you don't need to know what a paratha is to understand that it's something that goes well with eggs for breakfast. If you're really dying to know what a paratha is in detail, and you've never had one, Google will show you a picture, and even give you a recipe. And if you've never eaten a paratha, you really are missing out—I strongly recommend you rectify the situation post-haste.

Since the publication of my translation of Khadija Mastur's first novel, *The Women's Courtyard*, I've had the good fortune to discuss the book with many readers around the world, both in person and via social media. I have heard from many readers who are able to read Urdu, but haltingly, that they felt something was lost in the translation. And they are right! What's lost is Urdu, the mother tongue of many such readers. Khadija Mastur's Urdu is lovely and crisp. It is not difficult or flowery and ornate. If you find yourself nostalgic for Urdu while reading this translation, I urge you to put down the book and go online to the website *Rekhta.org*, where the entire novel, *Zameen*, is available for free electronically in a nice clean copy. Reacquaint yourself with the beauty that is the Urdu language and browse the website for short stories and poetry as well. You won't be disappointed.

But let us also remember that a literary translation is a work of creative writing in and of itself. We often talk about what is lost in translation, but we rarely discuss what is gained. I would argue that there is much to be gained. On a literary translators' forum on Facebook, one user asked the group a question: what metaphors have you heard of or do you think of to describe translation? There were hundreds of replies. I doubt any other profession would come up with so many metaphors for itself. A translator is like a musician, interpreting a particular piece of music that was written by a composer; no, translators are like cover bands; translation is like unravelling a sweater and re-knitting it into a pair of pants. And the funniest one: translation is like using a Lego instruction booklet to build a model, but using a different brand of building blocks. When someone posted the cover band metaphor, I said that I preferred to think of myself as Yo-Yo Ma playing Bach.

But of course that metaphor is imperfect too: really it's like I'm trying to play Indian classical music on a cello or a piano. It's going to come out sounding completely different, but it may still be a thing of beauty. The music metaphors resonate the most for me because translation is also an art form. Art, for me, is an alchemical process by which ideas and images and sounds, depending on the medium, enter the artist's psyche, and are transformed by their way of seeing and thinking. Translation is one such alchemical process practiced within highly formal constraints.

Daisy Rockwell

A
Promised
Land

1

'My daughter, my daughter! Where is my daughter?' the old man screamed as he tore at his hair. Then he bowed his head, as though he'd found peace in screaming. He sat in the same position for hours after that. Everyone tiptoed by him. No one spoke to him. No one responded to him. Perhaps no one had the strength, or they were all wrapped up in themselves, but his every scream pierced Sajidah's heart. She wished she could go and comfort him, but she couldn't stir from her spot. What could she say after all? What words could she speak to show sympathy to a father whose daughter must have been abducted? She was tired of hearing words like *patience*. She could not speak of patience to the old man. Whenever he screamed, Sajidah searched anxiously for the right words. She had no idea why words had not yet been invented for comforting victims of violence.

To calm herself, she avoided looking at him, but then her eyes darted about: all the women and men around her had an impoverished look. Everyone had found themselves a niche, whether in the long, discoloured, deserted army barracks, or under the shade of trees and makeshift roofs made of durries, or in the darkness of tents: they had found some shelter on that bit of land that had enfolded their exhausted feet in its bosom. Her father had also created walls beneath a dense tree using thick sheets and ushered her inside. There, she had sighed with relief for the first time after the horror of the journey.

This was their third evening at Walton Camp. The aid committees had distributed split chickpea dal and soft warm rotis right before sunset amid enthusiastic slogans in praise of God, and now bands of hookah-smokers sat about small campfires. At every hookah puff, a tiny cloud of smoke rose and disappeared into the air. People spoke loudly to one another, attempting to cheat the weight of their own hardships on the scales of distress. Groups of women sat apart. The filthy, wrinkled borders of their saris flapped in the cool breeze, and their faces bore the traces of deprivation from the protection of their former homes. The girls looked traumatized; nevertheless, they still covered their faces up to their foreheads when they saw young men walking by. It was only the children who were unmoved by worldly cares. They jumped and leapt about, as though it were Eid or Bakr Eid, and they were at home, in their own *gali*s. November was half gone, and it grew chilly the moment evening fell, but Sajidah couldn't tell it was winter from the look of things.

A child ran right by her, stepping on her foot. Perhaps the children were playing hide-and-seek. She stood up, rubbed her foot, and pulled the blanket they'd received in alms around her shoulders. Dinner was still laid out on the trunk. Abba wasn't feeling hungry, and she wasn't about to eat without him. She took a salvaged fourth-year course book from the trunk and went and sat cross-legged on the ground by the electric streetlight. She'd read only one line when a woman came and stood by her. She'd been pacing for a long time, patting her baby to sleep.

'Are you reading English or Urdu?' she asked.

'English.'

'What good will that do you?'

'No good,' she said apathetically, hoping to get rid of her.

'Where is your mother?'

'She passed away,' she said sadly.

'She passed away, tsk tsk! Are you married?'

'No!'

She bent over her book feigning deep concentration to avoid the woman, but every letter in the book became an S . . . *Salahuddin, Salahuddin, Sallu.*

She closed the book. The woman had gone away, perhaps thinking her arrogant.

2

Such memories had filled her heart with longing ever
since her arrival. Separation refreshes the memory; a slight
reminder can be traumatic. She recalled the first time she'd
met Salahuddin, when he'd told her, 'My name is Salahuddin,
but Amma calls me Sallu—everyone does. You can call me
that too.'

'All right,' she'd agreed dutifully. This had made him
happy, and he'd told her his entire life's story.

'We've come from a village, we have land there, and many
trees—mango trees—when they blossom, the cuckoos sing, and
when they eat the unripe fruit, I kill them with my slingshot.'

'How can you kill them?' she asked, alarmed.

'Ha! Killing isn't all that hard. It's just a cuckoo; people
kill other people too. Come, meet my Amma. So, yes, I came
here to study. My Abba made my Amma come with me. She
doesn't like it here.'

Then he flipped his hair self-importantly and went away.

Two nurses walked quickly by, carrying some packages.
They set them down by her for a moment.

'The population of our country has already grown,' said
one.

Then they continued on their way. Sajidah burst out laughing. Had they just stopped to announce this good news?

In the morning, she'd gone to the maternity centre for a little while. The new mothers lay moaning on bare rope beds, their newborns beside them, swaddled in their dupattas. Perhaps the baby clothes they'd sewn had been stolen somewhere along the way, or they'd forgotten about the coming birth of these small lives as they endeavoured to save their own. How could they have known that death and birth would jockey for attention with such momentous changes?

She stood where she was and scanned the groups of hookah-smokers in search of Abba.

The old man began to scream again: 'Where is my daughter? Where is my daughter? Bastards! Bring me my daughter!'

People looked up and around and then turned back to their hookahs. Sajidah felt restless and started walking towards him. But what could she say? What could he tell her? At that moment, she had nothing in mind. She was only a few steps away, when a man came up and placed his hands on the old man's shoulders.

'Baba! Who is this daughter you cry for? That was no daughter, Baba! That was the most valuable of looted goods. Your screaming won't bring her back. Your voice cannot reach her.'

The old man stared at him vacantly. Sajidah wished she could go up and slap the evil man across the face. She'd tell him that those who call women the spoils of looting, who are sarcastic about such things, do themselves no credit. But instead, she just stood by with silent restraint.

'You're lying,' the old man shrieked again. 'She was my daughter! She wasn't spoils or treasure. My daughter, my daughter!'

'Baba! Revenge has already been taken for the abduction of your daughter. Many fathers must be weeping like you on the other side too. If the looted goods are returned, the revenge won't be complete.'

'Aha,' said the old man, rolling up his sleeves. 'So, you've stolen daughters too?' He shoved the younger man so hard he nearly fell over. The younger man glanced at Sajidah and snickered.

'Baba! I can't comfort you. I can't reassure you,' he said, as though speaking to Sajidah. 'How can I make you understand . . . people are just spontaneously taking revenge. This is an ancient game, Baba! You have no idea how many blameless people have been destroyed by this game for centuries.'

What did the old man hear? How much had he understood? Now he shook his fists at the younger man in rage. The younger man walked away, head down, and disappeared into a group of hookah-smokers.

'Baba!' Sajidah called out softly as she approached him.

The old man looked at her as one might a stranger and then turned his back and sat down as though he didn't wish to speak to anyone now.

Sajidah set out for her spot, her heart filled with regret at not being able to say anything useful. When she passed a group of hookah-smokers she heard Abba's voice and stopped.

'Why are you wandering around over here, daughter?' he asked, taking a long puff on his hookah. He stood, wiping off his clothing. Now Sajidah saw that Abba was warmly shaking the hand of the young man who had been trying to console the old man by calling his daughter 'valuable spoils'.

She returned to their home with walls of sheets, sat down comfortably against the trunk and stretched out her legs. She was feeling exceptionally hungry now. *Perhaps Abba is sitting with his hookah again*, she thought. *I fear for his failing health if he keeps smoking his hookah on an empty stomach like this!*

She heard the last prayer of the night; voices grew softer, but the gramophone records continued to play after namaz, until ten or eleven at night. Night was when people spoke most exuberantly about their safe arrival in Pakistan. A few boys with good voices began to sing melodies. Sajidah didn't like any of this. She wanted privacy to think. She wanted to awaken her memories and feel embraced by fresh joy. But hearing the worn-out records every day, thousands of times, troubled the sweetness of her memories. At that moment, she felt as though even her own memories were just a worn-out record with a stuck needle.

When Abba returned with his small hookah, the younger man was with him.

'All right then, we'll meet again tomorrow, Nazim Sahib!'

'Goodnight,' said the man, and he left.

'Who is that, Abba? Is he from the galis of Delhi?' she asked.

'No, Sajjo, my daughter! Nazim Sahib is from Kanpur. An excellent man. The government here has hired him to work for the Department of Rehabilitation. What to say, he's wonderful—a very refined man.'

Abba seemed quite pleased.

'Have some roti, Abba!'

It made her sad to see Abba praising such a vulgar individual. Abba took an instant liking to anyone who spoke kindly to him.

Sajidah placed the dish of roti and dal before her father and took the hookah from his hand. Abba burst out laughing.

'My daughter has declared war on my hookah.'

'Please eat some roti, your stomach won't fill up on smoke alone.'

'I swear, daughter! I'm not hungry at all, I haven't even digested my afternoon roti yet. You eat now—if I get hungry in the middle of the night, I'll eat then.'

He rolled out his bedding and lay down. Eating alone was as bitter as poison to Sajidah.

'Abba! What village will we settle in? Where must Sargodha be? Let's move somewhere near Sargodha at least. What do you think, Abba? I'll teach children there at a school.'

'A village? And Sargodha! What on earth is there, crazy girl? What is there for us in a village?'

'Peace!'

Abba stared at his daughter in the dingy lantern light.

'My daughter feels tired; she's sad without a home. Eat your bread, then have a nice sleep. It just takes a while to get out of the camp. Once my daughter has started studying again, she'll be happy. I'll have you study up to the MA level.

What could possibly go wrong now? You've arrived in your own country.'

She looked sadly at Abba. He'd spent his entire life keeping accounts at a large shop for a low wage. What more could he dream of than having her study all the way to an MA degree? After that, he'd find a worthy son-in-law and that would be that. There were no numbers in the account book for hearts or emotions. How would she tell Abba why she wanted to settle in a village now?

Abba had fallen asleep and was snoring softly. She rolled out her own bedding and lay down. She could make out bits of sky among the branches. A nesting bird fluttered about, and a single leaf floated down to her. She picked it up and gently rubbed the soft leaf between her fingers. She thought for a moment about how this leaf was not yet completely dry. There was still some life in it. Reading the literary books Sallu had given her had made her more sensitive.

The onslaught of the gramophones had begun from all sides:

Come please, come, please come into my embrace again
Drip, drip rains the cloud, the intoxicating breezes blow
Sleep now, princess, sleep, my darling, sleep

'Turn it off, I'm going deaf listening to all these songs!' someone growled loudly. 'Throw out your records! Have you no shame playing them?'

All the records stopped at once as though they'd been snapped in two.

'Children! Play the songs of your own country.'

My lord, call me to Madina. Oh my lord! Call to me!

'Now that's really something . . . wonderful!' someone praised.

Sajidah leaned over and looked at Abba, hoping all this approval and disapproval had not woken him. But Abba slept deeply in the cool air. There was a lovely smile on his face; perhaps he was having a sweet dream.

She left me, after yanking her hem from my feeble hands . . .

This was the voice of a boy who was singing in a theatrical *nautanki* style. Sajidah listened carefully. She had heard this style as a child and liked it very much today.

'*Abey*, shut up! These wicked habits won't fly in Pakistan now. You were mad after nautanki there, and here as well.'

The singing stopped suddenly, and with that, everyone fell silent, because now the old man was shrieking again.

'I was left holding the ripped hem of her kameez. Where is my daughter? Where is she!'

Sajidah thought for a moment. What if she too had been abducted like the old man's daughter . . . Suddenly she felt horrified. She was terrified by the mere thought of it. How could she understand what it was like to break free from the poisonous jaws of violence, for which no antidote had yet been invented?

She imagined the old man as her own father and burst into tears, and when the heavy feeling had left her chest, she realized she was weeping for him. She felt some relief when she was done crying. Today, as she gazed up at the sky, she wondered why people called the sky a roof. If it was a roof, then why did humans feel so unprotected beneath it? As she fell into a deep sleep without a struggle, she missed the roof of her old home terribly.

3

She saw Salahuddin in her dream that night. She was getting ready to depart for Lahore, her bags packed, wandering about the camp, greeting people from her old street and neighbourhood. She asked each of them where they would go and expressed sympathy to those who were not leaving right away. As she comforted them, she noticed Sallu was there too, looking for something.

'You haven't left yet? How did you get here? Did you deliver your mother safely?'

'Don't worry about us. I've come to see you. Abba has decided we'll all go to Sargodha, or we'll live in a village nearby.'

'In a village in Sargodha?' she asked to reassure herself. 'We're going to Lahore.'

'Don't you worry. I'll become a lecturer at a college in the city.'

'But . . . but how will I know, Sallu?' she wept.

'Don't cry, I'll find you somewhere or other.' When he laughed, his dry lips cracked and began to bleed. She tried to wipe the blood away with her *pallu*, but Sallu suddenly disappeared.

Her eyes opened. It was a cold night, but she was bathed in sweat.

'I'll find you somewhere or other,' she whispered. She was astonished at how real a dream could seem!

From far off came the howling jackals. There was no hint of dawn breaking in the bits of sky peering through the branches. Someone was wandering about holding up a lantern. First the jackals, then a mysterious wanderer: her hair stood on end. She covered her face. She wished she could wake Abba, but she couldn't bring herself to speak. *It must be some vagrant, there was no way thieves had entered the camp,* she comforted herself. Then suddenly, the lantern light was filtering through the blanket and shining into her eyes. She pulled her blanket down slightly. A lantern swung before her. She closed her eyes and screamed with all her might.

'She's here, she's here—I heard her scream! My daughter, my daughter!' The old man's cries mingled with her screams.

Many people at the camp ran over to them when they heard the commotion. Then they went away again. She couldn't hear what they were saying; perhaps they were angry at being woken up. Abba placed a hand on Sajidah's head and glowered at the old man.

'You're causing a scene at night now too? Get out of here!'

Abba stared at the old man, who gazed at fearful Sajidah lost in thought. He paid no attention to what anyone was saying.

'Baba, I screamed, I was frightened!' she explained as she sat up in her bed.

'Do all girls scream the same way?'

'Yes, Baba!'

Sajidah reached out and placed her cold hand on his.

'I thought . . . I understood . . . are you very valuable goods?'

'Go on, Baba! Get away from here. Don't talk nonsense now,' said Abba. He placed his hand sternly on the old man's shoulder and the lantern fell from his hand.

'Pick up the lantern and put it away, daughter! Who knows who he took it from!' said Abba, practically dragging the old man away.

'Go lie down on your bed and go to sleep quietly. Your daughter will come in the morning.'

Abba took the old man away, muttering as he returned, 'He's gone mad, disturbing everyone's sleep.' He lay down on his bed. 'Go to sleep, daughter! Go to sleep. Half the night has already passed. May God let no man lose his mind.'

Sajidah did not reply to Abba. She didn't even look at him. She was still upset by the way he'd dragged the old man away.

Abba had gone to sleep but she couldn't sleep a wink. She watched the dark sky turn slowly white through the tangle of branches. She heard the clamour of birds as they fluttered away and felt strangely joyful at the sight of the tiny branches and leaves filtering through the blanket. She pulled the sheet wall to one side. Outside, people were bathing with *lota*s and small bowls.

'Abba! It's morning!' she called out softly.

Morning always looked lovely to her. Abba turned over and gazed at her affectionately.

'You're up? What were you doing, daughter?'

'Asking for blessings.'

'What blessings did you ask for?'

'Just general blessings, Abba,' she said, annoyed. 'All I said was, "Oh, Allah! Please forgive us our sins,"' she said automatically.

'What sort of a blessing is that, crazy girl?' asked Abba in a serious tone. 'How have we sinned? After your Amma left us, I heeded nothing else in the world as I raised you.'

Sajidah laughed after he went off to bathe with his lota. That was the blessing Abba always asked for himself, but when he'd heard it from her today, he took it as an insult.

After namaz, people were praying for all sorts of things. It seemed to Sajidah as though prayers for the welfare of the entire world fluttered in those outstretched palms. She thought of Amma. Although there were many things about Amma she'd completely forgotten, she still remembered some. Whenever Amma saw a loved one's head turned by wealth, she'd remark sadly, 'Maybe I'd understand if there were such a thing as edible gold.'

And Abba teased: 'At least humans can eat rich delicacies.'

But Abba was always pleased with Amma's contentment, and when she died, he wept and wept and told everyone that his contented wife had never made any demands on him.

Now the sleeping children had awoken and they rampaged about. Some cried. Some demanded food or drink and pulled at their mothers' saris. The women scolded and smacked them. One woman's voice rose above the others: 'Enough, you little devil! It's not as if we're staying! We've been living here three days eating charity rotis.'

Sajidah felt these words keenly. She began to think about how some people are never happy. They never try to feel deeply.

Why did they behave so ignorantly? She recalled those young men in filthy shalwars and kameezes who delivered hundreds of rupees worth of naan and food in cauldrons. Their faces shone with joy as they distributed the food. 'Pakistan is yours, brothers. We are your servants,' they told everyone.

Suddenly, a loud cry flew up from the children. Cauldrons of food and bags of naan were being unloaded from carts. The children promptly abandoned their mothers' sari borders and buzzed about the cauldrons like bees.

'Today, we've brought tea as well, *badshaho!*' called out a fair-skinned boy as though he were shouting a slogan. 'There's also haleem, *bhaiyo!*'

He then began corralling the children to one side. 'Just be patient, kids. The tea's grown cold.'

He quietly built a hearth from bricks, stuffed it full of dry branches, leaves and pieces of paper and lit a fire. As the tea warmed, he gathered the children around and began to dance cheerfully about.

'Drink tea, hot, hot! Eat roti, soft, soft!'

'Drink tea!' the children cried with him.

Sajidah found this all so sweet, she picked up a glass and ran towards the crowd. Breaking through the throng of children, she held out her own glass to the boy, who stood back bashfully.

'I will be the very first to drink the tea.'

'You can drink my portion of tea as well, Baji! I haven't even had mine yet.'

'Really?' she asked, looking at him affectionately. 'What's your name?'

'Ghulam Muhammad, but everyone calls me "Gamay." That's my nickname, Baji! And I brought this cauldron, too!

And I gathered the donations, even though people wouldn't give me any because they thought I was just a child,' he said, telling his entire story in one breath.

'Then this tea must be extra delicious.'

'Drink it and see, Baji!'

The boy filled her cup to the brim.

Sajidah had just come for the fun of it but when she saw people walking towards the cauldrons, she noticed there were no women among them. She ran back as fast as she'd come, and when she reached their spot, she saw that Abba had his *angocha* on his shoulder and was walking towards the cauldrons with his bowl and glass.

Sajidah sat down on the trunk and began drinking happily. The lukewarm tea boiled with *gur* overwhelmed her senses at that moment.

'I myself have never made such good tea,' she murmured, as though she were still chatting with the boy. She smiled cheerfully.

'I won't eat, I won't eat, where is my daughter! I heard her scream!'

She put down her glass. Her fleeting joy evaporated with the old man's screams. She wondered how long it had been since he'd eaten. She had no idea how anyone could console him. One man steals, another is sarcastic about stealing, a third goes mad from being robbed, and . . .

Abba was walking back jauntily carrying his food and drink. Was his carefree manner just for her benefit? *Abba is sad about losing his home, and he's doing his best to hide it,* she thought.

'Here you go, daughter! It's nice and warm. The most wonderful tea you'll ever taste. And look—there's haleem. They cook it all night long, just the way we make kichari.'

Sajidah picked up the glass using the end of her sari, poured half the tea into her own glass and handed his back to him.

'Abba, are you truly happy?'

'Yes, daughter! We've reached our country alive and well, why wouldn't I be happy!' He began to sip his tea.

'Then please eat a bit of naan. You didn't eat anything last night either.'

'No, daughter! You eat it. I feel as though someone has put a lid on my stomach. I just don't feel hungry.'

Sajidah looked hard at Abba, but he was drinking his tea peacefully. *He's not hungry,* she thought. Amma had saved every penny for twelve years and built them a two-room house out of bricks. She remembered when she was very young, how they'd lived in one small room with mud walls. When it rained, Amma spent the whole night moving things from one place to another, and Abba sneezed and sneezed as he tried to patch the holes in the roof, until he was exhausted and angry. Amma would make him tea and say soothingly, 'We won't live in this house forever.'

When they moved into their new home, Amma announced proudly, 'Look, Sajjo's father! I built us a palace, brick by brick!' She'd planted a motiya jasmine shrub outside her palace and trained a chameli vine up the wall and went about decorating in all different ways. But building and decorating her palace exhausted her so much that not long after, one rainy night in the month of Savan, she stretched out her legs and fell asleep so peacefully she never got up again. Abba quickly filled in for Amma. He rose when it was still dark, cleaned the house, made tea and toast and small thick rotis. Then he'd wake her affectionately, feed her breakfast, and when she was dressed and ready for school, he'd fasten the lock onto the door, drop her at school and go off to the shop. It wasn't long before she began to manage the house herself, and when Abba saw her cleaning, he'd get angry and say, 'This isn't your work, daughter! Am I getting you a bit of education so you can stoop to such tasks?' And she would feel sad. 'But then why do you stoop to them?' she'd ask. 'Abba! Don't say such things!'

In the evenings, when Abba returned from the shop, he'd wander about examining everything in the house, then water the motiya and chameli.

'Daughter! Who's been picking the leaves off this chameli?' Abba had asked her once.

She'd felt embarrassed and quietly turned away to work on some chore. How could she tell him that Sallu came to visit at night when Abba went to his friends' houses to smoke his hookah? And when she saw Sallu, she forgot all else and just started absentmindedly picking the leaves off the plant.

She turned to look at Abba again, but his flat face was expressionless. Really, how could it be that Abba wasn't missing their home? He couldn't stand the plucking of even one chameli leaf. He used to declare, 'I'll sign over the palace built by Sajjo's mother to my son-in-law, yes! He'll recognize my generosity and wash my daughter's feet and even drink the water from the washing.'

After Pakistan was created, the rioting picked up steam and their neighbourhood began to empty out too, but Abba still refused to leave. But when he realized their house was about to be invaded by not one, but ten sons-in-law, he left so fast he forgot to lock the door. At the refugee camp, he sat with his head down, mourning his palace, as he muttered, 'I built a palace, people, bit by bit—my home . . .'

Tears came to her eyes as she remembered this. She looked outside to escape the desolate memories of the past, and saw a large crowd gathering. She also noticed a doctor in the throng.

'Why are all those people gathering, Abba?'

'I don't know, daughter.' Abba cast a cursory glance outside. 'That tea has done my stomach a world of good,' he added.

'Good,' she said. She'd been holding her glass a long time, and now that she'd remembered it, it was cold.

'My daughter, my daughter!' screamed the old man. She could hear other people speaking too but she couldn't make out what they were saying from this distance.

'Abba! Go and see what's happening!' she said anxiously.

'What's to see, daughter! The poor thing has gone mad.' Abba began filling his chillum with tobacco. 'He'll quiet down soon. You're getting upset for no reason.'

With the last scream, the old man fell silent. People began to scatter. Everyone looked deadly serious. She felt the stillness that spreads after death.

'Abba, the old man hasn't died, has he? Everyone was gathered and now they're all leaving, why is that?'

'No reason, dear! I just saw him a little while ago. He was sitting comfortably under a tree. You spend too much time worrying about the whole world.'

Abba closed his eyes and began to puff on his hookah.

She felt angry at her father's indifference. She wished she could tell him, 'You just think of the old man as a book of accounts. Only sums are entered in that book, but never feelings.'

She went outside and looked around. Her eyes sought out the old man and the tree under which he sat silently for hours on end. Children played there now. Just then, she noticed Nazim walking swiftly towards her. When he drew near, she looked down indifferently.

'Where's your father?' he asked.

'What happened to that old man? People were gathered around him and he was screaming, and now I don't see him anywhere.'

'The doctor's sent him to the insane asylum. I heard he was harassing everyone last night. He frightened you as well?'

So Baba had been sent to the insane asylum. Those people had gathered to bid him farewell. She felt overwhelmed with sorrow. *Goodbye, Baba!* she said to herself. She was sad she hadn't been able to say goodbye. At that moment, it seemed impossible that Baba was already far away from all such things. His mind was a gramophone record filled with screams that would keep playing until the needle of his memory wore it down. Then the record of Baba's mind would be broken, and the insane asylum would get rid of him.

'Are you very sad? Maybe Baba will get better there. These insane asylums are made expressly for sensitive people. You also seem rather sensitive to me,' he added, and burst out laughing. Then he turned serious. 'What would happen if scientists made recordings of all the screams in the atmosphere? How would that make these civilized humans feel? They'd all run off to the jungles and dress in leaves, never to return.'

'Abba is inside,' she said. 'Abba! Nazim Sahib has come!'

She stepped away and began to look about. She didn't even notice the look of surprise on Nazim's face.

Abba jumped up and rushed out.

'Ah, so you've come. You're so considerate. People like you are hard to find. Please come in and take a seat,' said Abba, laughing foolishly.

'I'm in a hurry right now. I'll sit with you when I come tomorrow. Just give me the details for now. What did you leave behind?'

'Oh, oh, Nazim Sahib! Don't ask what I left behind. A five-room house, a huge fabric shop, and two munshis to keep accounts. Those were the days!' Abba sighed deeply.

Sajidah stared at her father in disbelief.

'I'm so sorry, Ramzan Sahib! I won't be able to get you a munshi,' Nazim laughed. 'For the time being, please take these papers, write out your claim and have two witnesses sign it.'

Sajidah stared at Nazim, her eyes glittering with rage, and then went and stood beside Abba. She wanted to tell Nazim, 'You've got some nerve making fun of my Abba!' But she couldn't say a word. Her legs trembled with rage.

Abba flipped through the papers and examined them.

'Forget one witness, I'll get four.'

'Okay, then, I'm going, I'll be back tomorrow.'

'Well, I really want to thank you. A man without a house is no better than a monkey.'

Sajidah felt that Abba was fawning over Nazim Sahib.

'Don't you worry, you'll get a home in a couple of days. I'll just break a lock and set you up.'

'Is that your job? Lock-breaking?' Sajidah's voice shook. This was the first time she'd ever had the nerve to speak to a man outside the family in front of Abba.

'The first time I broke a lock was when I came here,' he said seriously, without looking at Sajidah. 'All right then, goodbye, Ramzan Sahib!' And with that, he calmly walked away.

'You . . . you . . . Sajjo, my dear!' Abba burst out angrily. 'Did you really need to say such things? What need was there for you to interfere in men's conversations? Yes, you've stopped wearing a burqa but that doesn't mean—'

'Abba! What did I say to make you so angry? He was making fun of you and I got upset.'

'He was making fun of me? That was you who was making fun of me. Your tongue and feet have become too free. This morning, you went right into a crowd to get tea; last night, you showed the old man sympathy . . .'

She looked down and went inside. She knew that Abba was ashamed he'd made an accounting error today for the first time. She began to sob. Abba came inside a few moments later. Seeing her weep, he whimpered, 'Why are you crying, dear? I didn't say anything wrong to you. Are you angry with me? Don't cry, otherwise . . .' Abba's voice became tearful, '. . . otherwise I'll start crying as well.'

Sajidah quickly wiped away her tears. 'I'm not crying at your words, Abba! I just suddenly felt so sad.'

She looked up and smiled fondly at him. His face was flushed.

'It's just that I want you to be happy, my dear, and now look! There are only a few people here that we know from our old neighbourhood, and . . .' he picked up his cold hookah and began bubbling on it.

'Abba, please eat something.'

She gathered up the dishes, hoping to end the discussion. She felt pity for her father when she saw how ashamed he looked. He'd spent his life beating the drum of integrity, and that had forced him to live his whole life on very little means. And when he felt that no one knew him here he'd immediately ripped the skin off that drum. Now he sat with his head down, contemplating the dark shell that remained.

'Eat something, Abba!' she urged again.

He started as though roused from deep thought. 'Give me some roti.'

'It's been sitting right in front of you for ages.'

'Oh yes, I see, I didn't even notice. I'll just eat a little. I feel a slight pain in my stomach.'

'That's probably hunger pangs, Abba! All you've been eating is a couple of bites, that's it. You won't keep your health up this way. Today, you must go to the doctor.'

After she'd put away the dishes, she lay down on her bed. It made her extremely upset to see Abba so weak. And Sallu hadn't come yet either. Maybe he was coming with some other *kafila*, or perhaps he'd come by plane. If he came, she'd take Abba to a good doctor. Then, she remembered how Sallu used to share in her every sorrow and hardship. When she was ten or eleven and her mother had died, she'd been standing in the gali, sobbing, watching her mother's body depart and Sallu had come and lent her a shoulder.

'Don't cry, Munni! Don't cry,' he'd said, calming her like a man, and truly, she had quieted down. Sallu had come to see her several times a day, to distract her. He'd tell her stories of witches and ghosts and assure her that he had once seen a fairy with his own eyes, though she never believed him.

'Because why would a fairy come to live on the ground?' she'd ask.

Sallu would get annoyed and go away.

When she was studying in class seven, she took out Amma's dupatta and started covering her head, and from that time on, Abba scolded Sallu and told him he shouldn't come to the house any more. In those days, Sallu had taken the matric exam and gone home to his village, and she felt restless without him. She spent her time counting the days to the end of vacation.

Abba went to get medicine and returned. He drank a sip of water and then lay down.

'Abba, how are you feeling now?'

'Oh, I'm fine, dear.' He turned over and curled up, his knees nestled in his stomach.

'Abba, I'll massage your head. You'll sleep a little and then you'll feel better.'

She sat down by Abba's bed and softly massaged his temples. He closed his eyes and was soon snoring lightly.

That means the medicine helped, thought Sajidah with a sigh of relief. When two yellow leaves fell on Abba's bed, she took it as a sign that their fortunes would soon turn.

She stood up from the bed and went to her own. The afternoon felt desolate. She lay down and closed her eyes. *If only I could fall asleep,* she thought. *For just a short while, man is released from all his cares and his dreams are as sweet as ripe fruit.* She began to think of Salahuddin. Once, she had told

Sallu she couldn't sleep at night and he'd looked at her with great surprise.

'Then you don't love me, Sajjo,' he said. 'People always sleep deeply in the shadow of love. Their dreams are as sweet as ripe fruit.'

But today as she fell asleep thinking of him, she had the sense that worms crawled through that fruit. She felt she could still hear the screams of the old man, and then she began to scream along with him.

'What's wrong, dear?' Abba sat up on his bed and looked at her anxiously.

'What happened, Abba?'

She noticed she was dripping with sweat.

'Nothing at all. You were sleeping and making a strange sound as though you were trying to scream. Were you having a nightmare?'

'Yes, Abba, I was dreaming about our journey. About the attack on the train in the middle of the night,' she lied.

'But now you're in your own Pakistan, daughter! You can forget all those things.' Abba began to laugh. 'Your mother, may Allah make paradise her fate, never feared anything.'

'How is your pain now?' she asked. Abba looked pale.

'It's fine—give me another dose of the medicine. Your mother used to make me a digestive powder whenever I had stomach pain. She'd give me a small pinch and I'd get better right away.' Abba sighed deeply.

As she gave him his medicine, Sajidah wondered why Abba was thinking of Amma so much today. Usually, he never mentioned Amma out of concern for her feelings.

'Abba, tell me truly, you aren't in too much pain?'

'No, no, dear.' He stood up. 'I'll just take a stroll and then I'll feel fine. There's probably something interesting going on outside and that will make me feel better.'

After Abba picked up the hookah and went outside, she held out her hands in prayer to lessen the burden in her heart.

She went and stood outside. There was quite a bit of commotion in the camp. A few ladies, their faces covered in pink powder, wandered about asking women about their hardships. Some people were loading their luggage onto carts. There were also visitors come to see their near and dear ones. They embraced and wiped away tears of joy. A boy walked by her singing:

Those who are separated will meet if the Creator wishes . . .

Whom does that boy long to meet? Whom does he await? she wondered. *Everyone here is obsessed with waiting as though they're standing on a train platform.* She too stood waiting. So far, he had not come to find her.

4

She could see Abba strolling towards her from afar, stopping to chat with people along the way. He knew even the most insignificant details about the camp: how many people had come, how many had left, how many were about to leave, and where they were going. When he told her of a departure, his eyes sparkled.

'One day, we too will leave—very soon—do you hear me, darling? It's not like we'll stay here forever.'

The sun had set. The birds nesting in the trees squawked. She felt miserable. The ladies were now departing, and cauldrons of food were being unloaded from carts. The low-powered bulbs on the electric street lamps lit up like pus-filled boils. She noticed that Abba seemed to drag his feet as he made his way towards her. When she leapt up and went to him, he put his hand on her shoulder.

'Abba! You don't feel ill, do you?'

'I'm fine, dear! Completely fine. People are saying cauldrons of meat have been delivered today. Why don't you go grab a dish?'

'You go inside and lie down; I'll bring the food right away.'

'No, no, dear! You haven't seen how people are crowding around those cauldrons.' He began to laugh. 'All the meat will be gone. If I rest, you'll go hungry, and the gravy smells delicious!'

As he took his hand off of Sajidah's shoulder, he suddenly clutched his stomach and bent over, as though he might fall.

'Forget about the food! You come inside,' she said.

She felt her legs tremble as she supported him inside.

She helped him lie down and picked up the bottle of medicine, but he waved it away.

'Why, Abba?'

'I'm not getting anything out of that medicine, tell the doctor . . .' Abba grimaced.

'I'll go to the doctor, Abba! I'll bring him right away.'

She went outside and began running as fast as she could. She didn't even hear him calling after her, 'Stop, dear! First get some food and come back. I'm fine!'

She was out of breath when she reached the dispensary. The compounder was seated on a stool outside, relishing his bits of meat with naan. When she turned to go inside, he put out his hand to stop her.

'Doctor Sahib's gone for a walk, Bibi,' he told her after swallowing a mouthful.

'My father is very ill.' She looked at him imploringly. 'When the Doctor Sahib comes back, please tell him to come and see Munshi Ramzan Sahib.'

She'd delivered exactly the same message once before, to the doctor living in their gali. That night too, Abba had suddenly had terrible stomach pains. The doctor came after a few minutes and told him he should have an operation to remove his appendix. After the doctor had left, Abba laughed heartily.

'Tomorrow, the doctor will tell me to get a new stomach,' he joked.

Sajidah tried her best to get him to listen, but Abba refused to even consider an operation. Sometimes her father's poor education made her weep bitter tears.

She waited a few minutes for the doctor to return and then remembered that Abba was alone. But he was no longer alone when she returned. Many people were gathered around and the doctor stood there too, silently, his head down. When they saw Sajidah, they moved away from the bedside. The lantern by the head of Abba's bed was guttering.

'You're here—I was looking for you at the dispensary. How is Abba doing now?' She gazed at the doctor, her eyes full of hope. 'Abba is all right, isn't he? Who told you my Abba was ill?'

'When I saw him walking, I called out to him,' an elderly man said in a tearful voice.

'I was on duty; if I hadn't gone for a walk, then . . .' said the doctor, peering into Sajidah's terrified eyes. 'I feel responsible for this.'

'It's Allah's will, it's Allah's will,' several voices lamented in chorus. It was then that she realized that Abba had died, and with that, she went numb. She saw the doctor leave, saw the crowd disperse, and she drooped like a weak branch as several hands held her up.

When she came to, two middle-aged women slept beside her. They were sitting up, leaning against one another, and each held a section of the Quran open before her.

She sat up softly, slipped the sheet from Abba's face and raised the wick of the lantern. The cold, forlorn face seemed to whisper, *Alas, my daughter! There's been an error in the account book of life; now what will you do?*

She placed her cheek against his cold face and began to sob quietly so that no one would hear her weeping, and no one would belittle her sorrow by urging her to have patience. And when someone quietly lifted her head, dawn had already broken and the sound of the azan could be heard from far off.

The women peppered her with questions: 'Do you have any relatives, or no?' 'Who will you live with now?' 'Where will you go?'

To each of these, she shook her head.

'So what if you have no one? Have we died?' said one woman conceitedly.

'As long as I'm around, you are not alone,' said the other, placing a hand on Sajidah's head, making her feel as though Sallu was patting her with his strong hand. *Don't cry, Munni! Don't cry, Sajjo!* But their consolation seemed cold and unfeeling. She wished she could scream loudly, *Abba has died, Sallu!* She pushed the woman's hand away gently.

Now the sun's rays peered in through the crack in the sheet. She saw the tea and cauldrons being unloaded from carts. Then she heard Ghulam Muhammad's call: 'Hot tea! Drink tea, badshaho! Tea!'

He began to dance among the children, singing, 'Drink tea, hot-hot! Eat naan, soft-soft!'

Sajidah covered her ears with her hands. Such a difference between this morning and yesterday. Ghulam Mohammad's voice sounded dreadful today.

She understood everything when the camp's manager came with a cot and a few men and stood by her.

'Daughter . . .' the elderly manager began, but then he stopped.

'I have some money to pay for Abba's final attire,' she said, speaking clearly, and with great forbearance.

'I've only come to get permission from you, daughter. I don't want anything. Ramzan was like a brother to me. After he's been bathed, I'll bring you for the final viewing.'

She couldn't respond to the old man despite her best attempts. She reached out to the small box and then froze as the men lifted Abba while reciting the kalima and departed.

The sheets on one side of their enclosure had fallen. Both women wept softly as they held onto her, but her own eyes were dry as empty teacups. Now she only felt the menace of loneliness and worried for the future.

Ghulam Mohammad must have seen the body being carried out. Breaking through the throng of children, he came to Sajidah and stood before her quietly with his head bowed.

'Go on, young man! Go do your work!' said one of the women.

'Baji, did your father . . .?' Ghulam Muhammad couldn't finish his sentence.

'Yes, Gamo, my father has died.' As she spoke haltingly, she saw tears flowing from the uncouth boy's eyes, splashing onto his dirty collar. Those tears broke her own self-control.

'Patience, patience, don't cry,' one woman comforted.

'*Lo*, let the poor thing cry, what else can she do? She doesn't have any relatives to keep her company. Oh, what a tragedy!'

Sajidah fell silent. These words of sympathy felt like hammer blows to her.

'Baji! Come with me! I have a mother, we have a small home. I have no sister, I'll take care of you, I'll . . .'

'Goodness, boy! Have some sense. What will the world say if a young lady goes with you?'

'All right, forget it,' Gamo replied sadly. 'What will the world say! But Aunty, this is not the world, it's Pakistan, Pakistan, and this is my Baji, my Baji.'

'Gamo,' Sajidah said affectionately. 'Don't you worry about me. I can take care of myself,' she stated with great confidence. 'Go now! People must be waiting for their tea. *Drink tea, hot-hot! Eat naan, soft-soft!*'

She hid her face in her arms and began wiping away the tears. When she heard Gamo sobbing, she lifted her head, but he was already gone. The world—and Pakistan—were all jumbled in her mind.

All the stages of the end of life were now completed and evening was falling. Just a few dark wisps of cloud floated by, and the nesting birds squawked again. Their whistling did not inspire longing in her today, and their every call made her wince.

The women had got up and gone away for a while and then returned. At this moment, they both seemed deeply concerned for her future.

'What I say is, my younger brother-in-law is such a wonderful boy; I can't tell you enough about him! Everyone loves him. He had a huge jewellery shop in Kanpur, but then everything was stolen. But he'll get a shop here as well. We managed to escape with thirty–forty seers of gold under our clothing.' The woman told her everything there was to know about her goldsmith brother-in-law in just a few words.

'And my brother, mashallah, studied all the way to class twelve, but he got caught up in the rallies and processions back there. He declared he would only return to his studies once he got to Pakistan. What I'm saying is, he burnt the candle at both ends for the sake of Pakistan. Really, sister! So, he's the one who created Pakistan—may Allah make his life long—he's so handsome, you'll forget all hunger and thirst when you see his face.'

Sajidah stared at the two women in disbelief: she saw two leeches, just like the ones the hakim had once fixed to her mother's legs. She had run outside in fear when she saw how they puffed up as they sucked Amma's blood. But these leeches were much more dangerous, for they were dismantling her self-confidence.

5

Her mother used to tell her a story when she was little:

> *Once upon a time there was a king, a king of the same God as you and me. So, dear, this king had seven daughters. One day, the king called his seven daughters to his side and asked each in turn whose fate they depended on. Six of the daughters said, 'Respected father, I depend on your fate!' But the youngest one said, 'Respected father, I live my own fate!' The king was angered by this and he ordered his servants to carry her off to the jungle in the palanquin and leave her there. The youngest daughter wandered about the jungle, dismayed. There was neither bread to eat nor water to drink. But then, thanks be to God, it so happened that the small princess found some treasure and used it to build an enormous palace and—*

Her mother would not yet have finished this tale of self-assurance when Sajidah would burst out, 'Amma! I am the youngest daughter!' She had developed a great affection for the smallest daughter, and that was why she took over the housekeeping after Amma died, freeing her father from many worries. But now that Abba had sent her off to the jungle of

humans in a palanquin and abandoned her there, she'd lost
the strength to search for treasure.

'Sister, you don't have enough money to leave the camp
and buy two meals! One can't fill one's belly on learning,' the
goldsmith's sister-in-law proclaimed.

'Oh, my, how amazing,' the sister of the Creator of
Pakistan retorted. 'You think you can show off in front of me
just because you earn a bit of cash banging out adulterated gold?
My brother's right when he says one must flee ignoramuses
sure as the arrow flies from the bow.'

'I'll just have a look at your bow and arrow!' cried the
goldsmith's sister-in-law, rolling up her sleeves and waving
her hands in the air. Sajidah closed her eyes and screamed,
'Abba!' And again, 'Abba, Abba!'

Both women panicked and turned to comfort her.

'We said nothing—for God's sake, be quiet.'

'We said nothing; nothing will happen against your
will. It's not like we're forcing you to do anything! We just
thought—poor thing has no support, where will she go?'

She couldn't listen to any more of this talk; all she wanted
to do was scream and cry. Then she sensed that a crowd had
gathered around her. When she felt a soft hand on her head,
she fell silent and opened her eyes. She reached up and touched
it. She saw a modest-looking girl with large round eyes in the
midst of the crowd. The girl pulled her close and pressed her
to her bosom, and she felt like the youngest daughter of the
king who had finally found the treasure.

'I know everything; you're not alone any more,' said the
girl, hugging her so hard she felt she would melt into her
breast. 'Will you come with me now, Sajjo?'

She was surprised to hear her name and looked up at the girl questioningly.

'Who are you? What are you? Where will you take me?'

The girl gazed into her eyes affectionately and seemed to be trying to understand her questions.

'I know her, daughter. You can trust her; go with her. You're all alone. She'll take care of you,' said the camp's elderly manager who stood beside the girl.

'But, I . . .'

Just then her eye fell on the goldsmith's sister-in-law and she shrank back, rubbing her head on the girl's shoulder.

'Go with her, daughter! I'll bring your luggage,' urged the manager tearfully.

She walked forward, wrapped in the girl's arms. She turned once and gazed back at the dense tree. It looked leafless to her, robbed of its treasures. Women, men and children all watched as she left, as though bidding her farewell.

She lay senseless, her face hidden in the girl's lap. They were seated in the backseat of a long, old car, driving noisily along a bumpy street. The girl stroked her head, and called out softly, 'Nazim bhai, drive slowly. We don't want to get in an accident.'

Sajidah jerked her head up. There was a snake coiled over the treasure trove she'd found. She wished she could jump out of the moving car and run away. She looked up at the girl helplessly.

'You should lie down. You're getting a headache from all that crying,' said the girl, resting Sajidah's head affectionately against her shoulder. Sajidah burst out sobbing. She was leaving the camp with the man who had made fun of her father and who had broken his first lock on arriving in Pakistan.

'You can't even comfort her, Saleema! I'm an inexperienced driver. What if we get into an accident?' Nazim sped up the car. 'When my brother finds the car missing, he'll be extremely displeased.'

Sajidah wiped away her tears and looked out the closed window. There was no light on the tree-lined street. The clouds made it seem darker. And now she was worrying that Sallu would come looking for her at the camp. When he didn't find her there, he'd ask people, he'd talk to the elderly manager, and he'd get word of her whereabouts from him.

The dark road had come to an end. Now both sides of the street were lit by electric street lamps. The car entered the gate of a mansion and came to stand in the porte-cochère. In the bright light, she could see that the paint was peeling; it looked extremely old. The tall trees lining the lawn spoke of bygone years and the scent of roses filled the air.

When she got out of the car, she felt a chill and shivered. Nazim disappeared as soon as he got out of the car. Saleema took Sajidah's cold hand and led her through the large front door. Her feet sank into the thick carpet covering the hallway. For a moment, she stood still.

'What's wrong, Sajjo?'

'I'm tired,' she said softly.

'Tired after walking such a short distance?' the girl smiled.

'I've travelled a very great distance, Baji!' said Sajidah tearfully. At that moment, she heard a high voice coming from the open doors of the next room.

'You think this is some kind of halfway house! You don't even consider your poor, exhausted father. First, your mother picked up Taji on the pretext of getting housework done and now you. Do you even know how expensive flour is right now?'

'Can't you keep it down? Just because you rule over one person you seem to think everyone here is your slave.' This was Nazim speaking. Saleema began to pull Sajidah along.

'You're already so tired, Sajjo! Walk quickly. You can rest in your own room for a while, then you'll soon feel refreshed.'

Thick carpet. Halfway house. Expensive flour. Oh, Allah, what place is this! How can all these things exist side by side?

'Saleema, my daughter! Where are you, my darling?' Now the high-pitched voice echoed in the hallway.

'I'm coming, Ammi!' Saleema turned and called back, before leading Sajidah into a small, abandoned room where a string bed with colourfully painted legs invited her to rest.

'Saleema Baji,' Sajidah stared at Saleema vacantly.

'You rest now, Sajjo. Taji will make tea for you right away. In the morning, she'll clean up your room and bring in your luggage. When it's time to eat, I'll come and get you and introduce you to everybody. Okay?' Saleema looked at her innocently and then went away, smiling.

Sajidah heard the sound of distant thunder. A brisk breeze blew in through the open window. She got up and closed it and then sat down on the bed with her feet dangling. Her head was exploding with pain. At this moment, her entire capacity for thinking and understanding was melting into pain.

'Here, have some tea, and here's your bedding,' said a girl entering the room. The girl placed the bedroll on the bed and handed her a cup of tea.

'Are you Taji?' asked Sajidah, staring at the tall, rangy girl. She was rough around the edges but looked innocent.

'Yes, I'm Taji.' She smiled. 'It's good you came. I get so tired doing all the housework for such a large home.'

'Taji, tell Saleema Baji that I won't eat, all right? Will you do that, so she won't trouble herself coming to get me?'

'Oh, my!' Taji laughed loudly.

'What's so funny?' asked Sajidah, glaring at her. Then she fell silent.

'Bring the cup back yourself. I'm going,' said Taji, glaring at her before leaving.

Sajidah got up and locked the door with the chain. She made up the bed hastily, put out the light and lay down. She had no idea when she finally fell asleep as she moaned with intense pain.

6

The next day she awoke at dawn. The house felt deserted and still it filled her with despair. Long brown cobwebs hung about her room. Dust coated the door, the windowpanes and the large niches built into the walls, where colourful designs could be glimpsed through the hazy layers of grime. A few broken clay lamps lay scattered about the floor, their half-burnt wicks like long brown worms. It seemed as though no human hand had touched the room in ages.

She grew tired of lying in bed and stood up, but she had no idea what she should do. She went and opened the window just for the sake of it and glanced outside. Someone was strolling briskly—almost running—around the edge of the unkempt lawn. She saw that the man had salt-and-pepper hair, and she thought of Abba, who also used to take walks in this manner. The only difference was that he strolled through galis and lanes, and here, there was a lawn. She hoped sadly that this man did not suffer from a stomach ailment as well.

Through the mist of her tears she felt she saw her own father strolling on the lawn, and she leaned against the window frame.

There was a knock on the door.

'Who is it?'

'It's me, Taji.'

She wiped away her tears and opened the door. Taji stood before her, one hand on her waist. She was smiling and looked extremely cheerful.

'What is it, Taji?' she asked, irritated at her smile.

'Were you cleaning the room with your hair?' Taji asked, giggling. 'It's full of dust.'

Sajidah brushed off her hair with the pallu of her sari and grinned foolishly.

'Where is the bathroom, Taji?'

'There's a nice big bathroom next to the servants' quarters. If you want to bathe there, you'll enjoy it. But first, come with me and cook breakfast, then you can wash up.'

Taji spoke with such seriousness that Sajidah felt momentarily confused.

'Taji! You think I've come here to do housework!' she snapped. Then, calming herself, she explained softly, 'Saleema Baji has brought me here as a sister. Do you understand?'

'Well, la-di-da,' laughed Taji harshly. Then she turned serious. 'When the older mistress brought me here from the camp, she said she would keep me as her daughter because she didn't have one. I called her Amma. But do you know what happened? Saleema Baji's mother turned me into the servant of this house. All I get for pay is food and clothing. She made me her daughter while quietly planning all this. Now I don't call her Amma any more.' A tiny spark flared in Taji's eyes, and then it died. It was a spark of vengeance. She laughed again. 'Now, you come with me; no more games.'

Taji casually grabbed Sajidah by the hand and pulled her along.

'Get out of my room!' screamed Sajidah in horror. 'The person who will make me a servant is not yet born. I'm leaving. Where is Saleema Baji? I'll ask her. Go and bring her here.'

She shook from head to toe as Taji shrank back, staring at her fearfully. Just then, Saleema appeared, out of breath. She must have been running.

'What's wrong, Sajjo, why were you screaming?' she asked. 'What's happened, my darling?' Sajidah trembled as she held her tightly. 'Taji! Did you do something rude? You've become very cocky these days.'

'All I said was "Come cook breakfast with me." That was enough to make her start screaming,' she replied tearfully. 'Everyone makes me work all the time. I never scream, never . . .' She wept, her face turning copper-red.

Sajidah's heart was warmed by her honesty.

'Taji is being honest. What she said made me scream.'

'Idiot! You rude little . . .' Saleema said angrily. 'Taji! If you ever say such things again . . . You remember, yes—this is your Sajidah Baji. She's not like you, she's very educated. Do you understand? She's like me.'

'I see!' Taji looked at Sajidah doubtfully.

'Come now, go get breakfast ready quickly. If it's late, Malik will get angry.'

Taji walked away silently with her head down. Saleema heaved a sigh of relief.

'She's just so crazy, Sajjo! Don't worry about the things she says. Now come along and I'll show you my bathroom. Your clothes have become so dirty; you wear one of my saris today. After lunch, Taji will clean your room, then she'll arrange your luggage. Is that all right?'

She put her arm around Sajidah's waist affectionately. But as Sajidah walked along with her, she felt as though she wasn't moving of her own accord: if Saleema were to remove her arm, she'd fall with a thud. Her body hadn't stopped shaking; Taji's words still tormented her.

'Saleema Baji . . .'

'Yes, what is it?'

'Why . . .' Sajidah found it difficult to speak.

'Tell me, what is it?'

'. . . why have you brought me here? I mean, why?'

'That's it? Such a little thing to ask! You've come here to protect your future. Nazim Bhai said that you're free to do whatever you want. He'll help you in every way to become what you wish.'

'He'll help me?' Sajidah laughed sarcastically, but Saleema didn't seem to notice.

'Yes! He'll help you. When Nazim Bhai found out that your father . . .'

Saleema fell silent.

'When Abba died, Saleema Baji, a crowd of helpers gathered around me.' She shut her eyes for a moment and her lips began to tremble softly. 'But Gamo was not among them, he had left—*Drink tea, hot-hot! Eat naan, soft-soft!*'

When she opened her eyes, she was standing by the door of the room and Saleema was staring at her.

'What can you be thinking, Sajjo! I think you're misunderstanding. Nazim Bhai told me you were very intelligent, but that if intelligence is pushed into misfortune, it dies—and—and he said lots of other stuff as well. He said that people were nothing if they were alone. Every person's joys and sorrows are connected with everyone else's, and who knows what all he was saying . . . I don't remember now.'

'Yes, Baji! My intelligence should not die,' she said with a mournful laugh.

'All your doubts will disappear if you stay a while.'

Saleema led her into the room. Sajidah looked about, feeling lost. She was thinking about all the intelligent people at the camp whom no one had noticed. Even those in search of intelligence had gone blind. But perhaps even the blind can discern a helpless girl's intelligence...

'Why are you looking at my room so sadly?' asked Saleema, pressing her hand.

'No, I'm not . . .' she replied, startled. 'It's really lovely, Baji. The rooms in tales of fairies and jinns are decorated just like this. If a beautiful daughter of Eve lived here and a jinn fell in love with her and carried her off . . .'

Saleema laughed loudly. 'You're too much, Sajjo! Your memory is so good—I've forgotten all those stories. All right, now go ahead and change your clothes.' Saleema opened her wardrobe, pulled out a sari and blouse and stuffed them into her hands.

'But Baji! My clothes . . .'

'Don't worry about them. I'll wear your clothes too. Just get ready quickly.'

Saleema pushed Sajidah affectionately towards the bathroom.

You'll wear my saris? They're five- and six-rupee cotton saris. They would make your skin itch, she thought as she flipped over the silk sari to examine it. Then she sat down on the stool to bathe.

The whole time she bathed, she wondered how long she would stay there. She had no idea what life would be like if she stayed. Would she complete her education? Would she become independent? Some kind person wanted her intelligence to survive, but who was he? He wasn't related to her, they shared no ties; there was nothing between them but a wall of hatred. As she considered this, she burst out weeping, her hot tears dissolving in the cold water.

She felt much lighter when she'd cried her heart out. She encouraged herself with the thought that she was Sajidah, and that no one could turn her into a Taji. She wondered how many days had passed so far as she dried her wet hair with a towel and brushed it back. She was convinced that Sallu would find her . . . 'I'll find you, somewhere or other,' she sang softly, and when she emerged from the bathroom, she was smiling.

'Oh no, were you crying? Your eyes are swollen,' asked Saleema, examining her carefully.

'No, the water was very cold,' she replied calmly.

'Come then, let's get breakfast. If we're late, Malik will get angry. He's very punctual.'

'Who is Malik, Saleema Baji?'

'He's my uncle, but Ammi always calls him Malik, so all of us children also got into the habit, and . . .'

Sajidah hesitated at the dining room door. The breakfast things were set out on the table and two women, one plump and one skinny, were there with Nazim, along with another young man who was rather handsome with curly hair, and a heavy middle-aged man. They were all seated about the table on chairs, chatting loudly. As soon as they saw her, they fell silent and stared, their eyes boring into her face.

'Come, come in, why are you hesitating?' Saleema whispered to her.

'I feel frightened of this palace of yours, and its inhabitants.'

'So silly, you're making it seem like someone carried you off from a shack. Nazim Bhai has told everyone that your father had two fabric shops in Delhi, with two munshis working at each,' scolded Saleema.

'Come on in, girls. Are you frightened of me? I don't bite!' called out the middle-aged man, chuckling at his own joke.

'I'm not afraid, Malik! It's only Sajidah that is,' laughed Saleema.

The plump woman gazed at Sajidah critically. Sajidah looked down and sat on the chair next to Saleema.

There were cut-up pieces of omelette and a paratha on each flowered plate.

'Haven't you learned how to say hello?' asked the plump woman sarcastically.

Sajidah stayed just as she was, as though she'd heard nothing.

'Ammi! You do know that this is the third day after Sajidah's father's death? She's very sad,' said Saleema, giving her mother a serious look.

Sajidah felt like crying but she held back her tears. She looked up once and stared hard at Saleema's mother. She was beautiful, but there was a strange rigidity to her face. She wondered how the mother of an emotional, shy-faced girl could look like that.

'Everyone dies eventually, darling!' said the skinny woman. 'Death is very real, but you shouldn't become the living dead. You must have patience.'

There was sympathy in her tone. She was small and weak, with a wheat-coloured complexion and sharp features clouded by the sort of desolation one hears in the cries of jackals on long, cold nights.

A hint of annoyance blew across Malik's face like a puff of breeze, then disappeared.

'No time for sorrow, Begum,' he said, addressing the skinny woman. 'Refugees have many troubles. Their homes are looted, their fortunes reduced to rubble. Now look around you, see how little we've got after coming here!' lamented Malik.

'How little we've got?' asked Nazim, practically jumping from his seat, but then he sat back calmly. 'Yes, we've got so little, nothing but this mansion on half an acre of land and everything in it. We've got so little; thankfully, before we left home, you sold your property to Krishna Sahib at a suitable price. How could all that stuff have fit in here? It would all have been ruined.'

Nazim's tone was razor-sharp.

For a moment, everyone was silent as they elegantly broke off tiny pieces of their parathas.

'Well, was that stuff really sold off at an appropriate price? What I'm sad about is that I didn't even get to taste one season of fruit from our mango orchard. And the bungalow we built with it. We weren't fated to stay there for even a day. The pension orders had come; I'd imagined I would spend the rest of my days peacefully in the shadow of my orchard.' Malik sighed deeply.

'Oh, Malik! Where on earth did this orchard and bungalow come from? Now I'm discovering that you hide everything from your own sons,' said Nazim, swallowing his food as though it was stuck in his throat.

'Such things are not told to adversaries,' chuckled Kazim. 'But I'm actually surprised to hear this as well.'

'Well, then we must be related,' said Nazim, glancing sideways at Kazim.

'The first thing you must do is prepare your claim, Malik. We should be awarded an orchard for an orchard,' said Kazim seriously.

'The real tragedy is that I've not seen any orchards here with locks on them, otherwise I'd have broken one long ago and turned it over to Malik,' remarked Nazim with a bold laugh. Malik chuckled hollowly along with him.

'But listen, brother,' responded Kazim in a serious tone. 'Your jokes will accomplish nothing. If Pakistan is to be made strong, the first thing the government needs to do is to take care of the refugees' problems.'

'By now, approximately more than a crore of refugees have already arrived!' interjected Saleema's mother, looking up at Malik smartly. 'Isn't that what you said? I was right, wasn't I, Malik, when I said that was quite worrisome?'

'Absolutely correct. And of course, we're the real refugees; the rest are just poor people who lived in huts back there as well. They slept on footpaths or the platforms of makeshift shops—people like that will just go ahead and make their own space here. When the government raises slogans about rehabilitation, they're really talking about people like us,' said Nazim in such a serious tone that Malik, Saleema's mother and Kazim all began to look angry. But Saleema was smiling for some reason.

'Oh, I get it. I get what you're going after, brother. I understand what you're saying full well!' yelled Kazim.

'Be silent. You two always disrupt the dining table,' Malik interjected bitterly. Both brothers put their heads down and finished their parathas in a few bites.

'Malik! Don't get angry with the children, it makes me sad. After all, I raised them,' said Saleema's mother after a few moments of silence. Then she began to fix Malik's tea.

Nazim's mother glared at Saleema's mother as if to say that anyone who claims to love more than a mother is a manipulative witch.

Sajidah was trying to understand everyone, trying to make sense of their personalities, but she could think of nothing except how everyone else's accounting had also gone wrong after they'd become refugees, and that the one responsible for those errors was Nazim. She missed her father keenly at that moment.

'Last night I had a dream . . .' Nazim's mother began, but she hadn't even finished her sentence when Nazim interrupted her.

'A dream! Please make sure not to dream, Amma! Dreams are worthless.'

Malik smiled slightly, and Sajidah wished she could get up and claw at Nazim's face. *What sort of a man doesn't allow his own mother to savour the sweetness of dreams?*

'You don't want anything else, Malik?' asked Taji, who had snuck up behind Saleema's chair at some point.

'No,' Malik replied softly.

Sajidah turned to look at Taji. Her eyes were pink, her lashes were damp, and her cheeks still shone with tears. Taji shot Sajidah a hard look and rushed away. After she left, Sajidah's heart felt heavy. She wished she could call out to her and assure her that she would help her prepare breakfast after all, that they would cook together.

'What kind of work did your father do, Sajidah Bibi?' asked Malik as though bored by the silence.

As Sajidah lifted her head to reply, Nazim, who sat across the table from her, gave her a look as though urging her to lie. She hesitated for a moment.

'Her father had fabric shops in Delhi and he—' Nazim began, but he couldn't finish his sentence.

'My father . . .' Sajidah interrupted Nazim with a sad sigh, '. . . my father was a munshi at a fabric shop. He worked his entire life at the same shop. He never made an error in his accounting, but after meeting Nazim Sahib, his accounting went all wrong, and . . .' She became tearful as she felt a heavy cloud of silence envelope the room. All eyes turned to Nazim.

'Wonderful!' exclaimed Kazim, chuckling heartily. The cloud evaporated.

'Truly, you should laugh. Unlike us, Sajidah Bibi refuses to be seen as a refugee. That should serve as a lesson to you,' said Nazim, glaring at Kazim.

Sajidah drank her last sip of tea and stood up. She had only just pushed her chair back when Saleema's mother stopped her.

'Sajidah Bibi, why don't you go ahead and clear the table with Taji. The poor thing is exhausted from doing all the work on her own.'

'In our home, one must immediately pay the price for truthfulness, Sajidah Bibi,' said Nazim softly.

'I have sacrificed my entire life for the happiness of this household, but no one has ever understood,' cried Saleema's mother, her face flushed.

Saleema glared at her with disdain.

'I have been told that if I stay here, I will finish my education. As for the dishes, Khala Bi, will you please clear them with me? I am not Taji.'

She left the room quickly. The din of raised voices followed her out.

She went into her abandoned room and sat on the bed. At that moment, she felt satisfied with her honesty and her insurrection. For a moment, she wondered what all of them must be saying. Surely they were talking about her. At the very least, they must have realized that they could not start an army of domestic servants by tricking destitute girls from the camp into thinking they'd be helped.

She jumped up excitedly and began to pace about, her sandals leaving footprints on the dust-covered floor. Suddenly, she remembered that when she was small, she used to walk about the courtyard barefoot right after it had rained and proudly count her footsteps. In a day or two, the courtyard would dry out and Amma would get out her bamboo-spiked broom and begin rubbing out all the footprints. At this, Sajidah would weep angrily.

'Oh, you crazy girl!' Amma chided. 'No one's footprints last on this earth. Dust storms and rains wipe them all away.'

She thought about how these footprints too would be wiped away when this room was cleaned. But why wouldn't the signs of love disappear as easily as footprints? And where could Salahuddin be now? He who had come to find her in the camp in that pandemonium of fire and blood. Wouldn't he be looking for her now?

To distract herself, she stood by the window. Pink roses peeked out here and there on the abandoned lawn. Several bricks had fallen from the enclosing wall and a thick tree branch leaned against it. The grass had grown so tall that the lawn was beginning to look like a field.

At that moment, she felt overwhelmed by pessimism, but that ended with the sound of a car starting. Kazim was backing towards the gate. When he'd got through, he waved a hand, and Sajidah suddenly felt embarrassed and stepped back. Had he seen her and waved? She wondered momentarily, but the next instant, Taji ran to close the gate and then ran off again. A little while later, Nazim appeared, pushing a bicycle. He opened the gate and went out. A few minutes after that, a tonga hitched to a gaunt horse entered through the gate. The elderly driver coughed as if to announce his arrival and then began to slap the horse quite hard. Shortly thereafter, Saleema emerged with her books and sat down in the tonga, genteelly covering her head.

Now the gate hung open like a pair of wistful eyes, but no one came to close it.

She grew bored and moved away from the window. She felt extremely sad now. After all, how long could she just stay sitting in this room? Saleema had gone to college—who knew when she would return—and everyone else here was a stranger. Even if she left the room, to whom would she speak? She had no idea what everyone thought of her.

For the first time, she realized her error; she shouldn't have been so confrontational. A person can learn to tolerate a great deal over time. She had no idea how Saleema would behave towards her now.

Just then, Taji came stomping in with a broom and a small basket.

'I've decided I'll clean your room first, Sajidah Bibi, then I'll start cooking. You must be so upset sitting in all this dust!'

'Taji, you're so nice! You're not angry with me?' asked Sajidah, remembering Taji's hate-filled eyes at breakfast.

'Oh no, Baji! What are you talking about? Do servant girls get angry at anyone?' she took her dupatta off and wrapped it around her head.

'Taji, you go and cook. Give me the broom. I'll clean my own room; I used to clean our entire house.'

Sajidah tried to take the broom from her hand, but Taji began to laugh uproariously.

'If you clean your room yourself, Nazim Miyan and Saleema Baji will take this broom and sweep me right out of the house into the trash. As she was leaving, Saleema Baji said that I was to clean this room the very first of all,' she added helplessly.

Sajidah breathed a sigh of relief when she learned that Saleema was not angry with her and that Nazim had also tolerated the embarrassment.

'Taji, I'll clean my room myself,' said Sajidah affectionately.

'No, no! You go on, Baji.'

Taji grasped Sajidah by the shoulder and pushed her out of the room.

'Just stand out here for a bit. I'll clean the room quickly. If you stay in here, you'll get covered in dust,' she said, closing the room from inside.

Sajidah looked about as she stood outside the room. Colourful curtains that had lost their shine hung in the doorways along the hallway. They looked as though they hadn't been washed for some time. Artificial flowers were arranged in a brass vase atop a wooden stand in one corner of the hallway. Everything had a musty look about it in the light of day.

She wished she could wander through all the rooms. She wondered who slept where, and what everyone was doing right now, and she wondered why she'd liked Nazim's mother so much.

'What are you doing here?' asked Saleema's mother, emerging from behind a curtain. She hesitated when she saw Sajidah standing in the hall.

'Taji is cleaning the room,' Sajidah replied softly. 'She told me to stay out here. Khala Bi, I wanted to clean my room myself, but Taji wouldn't listen.'

'I know perfectly well—that must have been my daughter's order. You can rest here for now,' she said sarcastically.

She walked away quickly and disappeared into another room. Sajidah was left anxious and at a loss for words. 'Allah! How will I live with these people and for how long?' she asked softly. She leaned against the wall and closed her eyes.

'Come on in, Sajidah Baji!' called Taji, opening the door. 'Come see how quickly I cleaned everything.'

'Yes, Taji! You've done an amazing job,' she said, looking at her affectionately. 'And my luggage?'

'I'll bring it in after I cook. It's in my quarters,' said Taji, as she picked up her basket of trash and turned to leave.

'Taji! What is his name, the one that left in the car, and then you closed the gate?' asked Sajidah.

'Kazim Miyan,' replied Taji, glancing at Sajidah proudly. 'He's Nazim Miyan's brother, the one who brought you from the camp,' she added mischievously.

Sajidah wished she could act like a child playing in a dirty gali and scream some horrible curse word at Taji, but she forbore and began to look about the room. Now, the painted flowers and the face of a deity were clearly visible in a niche once used for puja. She began to wonder how she would pass the time in this room now that Taji had left.

7

Everyone was present at the dinner table that night. Malik and Kazim were in excellent spirits. Saleema's mother gazed around affectionately at everyone but Sajidah as she served the platters of meat and gravy.

'This is too much, no one is eating anything at all. You're all eating like birds. And you, Sabirah Baji?' She looked at Nazim's mother fondly as though she wished to smother her with love. 'I guess I'll just have to force-feed you!' She placed two or three chunks of meat on Nazim's mother's plate.

Ah, so her name is Sabirah, thought Sajidah, as she glanced at Nazim's mother. *She looks like a Sabirah, so patient. I wonder if people's names shape their faces?*

'Eat, won't you, Begum!' urged Malik, looking rather pleased.

'How are your studies going, Saleema?' asked Nazim's mother softly as though she did not wish to reply to Malik.

'Fine, Khala Jaan.'

Sajidah noticed she had pushed the chunks of meat to one side of her plate. She glanced at Nazim who was deep in thought as he ate.

'Is something bothering you, Nazim?' asked Malik.

Nazim started. 'Nothing at all.'

'It's the sorrows of the age that bother the poor fellow. What else could it be?' teased Kazim carelessly. Malik and Saleema's mother laughed, as did Sajidah. But when she saw the serious look on Saleema's face, she felt flustered.

'You're such a fool, it's hard to imagine you're my own brother. Your only world is your tribe,' retorted Nazim with annoyance.

'One should only say nice things at the dinner table,' scolded Malik.

'You have no connection to my tribe, brother! You wander about, pockets empty, in the imaginary market of humanism. My life's goal is the pursuit of fun and joy,' countered Kazim contemptuously.

'And why should you have a monopoly on fun and joy, Kazim?' laughed Saleema.

'Oh! Saleema Baji!' he chuckled sarcastically. 'My dear brother here has poisoned your thinking as well.'

'Speak less, Kazim! Whatever I am, I am. No one can make me anything I'm not. Your heart is full of scorn for women,' said Saleema, turning her face away in anger. She began to eat as though her dinner were poison.

'No need to get angry, Saleema Baji. You'll agree with me when I've finished my MA and taken the CSP exam.'

'May God bring that day,' prayed Saleema's mother, raising her hands to ask for blessings.

'Please do not ask for such curses during dinner, Khala Bi!' said Nazim laughing. 'Or He'll grab your dinner and eat it all up.'

Saleema laughed loudly, but an uneasy silence hung about the room. Everyone appeared to be in a bad mood.

Only Nazim's mother, seemingly disconnected from all these topics, ate quietly. Sajidah found it difficult to understand everyone.

'You don't need anything else, Malik?' asked Taji, coming in and standing by him politely, her head down.

'You didn't cook from the heart today, Taji!' laughed Kazim. 'Well, when I become an important officer, you won't have to work this hard. I'll hire loads of servants and they'll all dance to your orders. And then you'll never cook such boring food again.' Kazim was acting like a small child and everyone laughed.

'May Allah bring you happiness, Kazim Miyan! When things get better, I hope there will never come a day when your servants consider me their servant.'

'Go on, go on, do your work. You're getting quite a sharp tongue in your head,' scolded Saleema's mother, and Taji began to clear the empty plates with her head down.

'That day may come, if my brother keeps bringing home servants,' suggested Kazim, giving Nazim a sidelong glance.

Sajidah began to tremble. Kazim and Taji's taunts had been sharp pinches, and she felt she would pass out with pain. She put her food back down on her plate. Tears flowed from her eyes and down her cheeks. Everyone stared at her.

'You leave the room, Taji!' Saleema shouted.

Taji shrank back and left the room. Everyone was silent.

'It's nothing, Sajidah dear. Just a bit of teasing,' offered Malik softly and haltingly as though he were afraid of her.

'And Saleema Baji, is this your humanity, to scold a poor girl so harshly?' snapped Kazim.

'I would scold you too if it would have any impact, Kazim!' wept Saleema.

'I feel as though my sons have lost their manners since coming to Pakistan,' said Malik in a serious tone.

'This is a man who equates manners with mango orchards,' muttered Nazim, before leaving the room quickly.

Malik gazed after him in astonishment.

8

When she returned unsteadily to her room, Sajidah saw that her things had been arranged prettily and her bed made. She turned out the light, lay face down on the bed and soaked her pillow with tears. As she wept, she called out softly to her father, as though he were somewhere nearby.

ଓ

'Sajidah! Why are you lying in the dark? Did you go to sleep already?'

Saleema turned on the light and sat down beside her. She lifted Sajidah's face.

'Oh dear! Look, you've cried so much. What a state you've put yourself in! Silly, how can anyone cry so much?'

'I was missing Abba, so today I cried my heart out. I'm worried about how I would live my life. I hadn't had time to cry before.'

'I know. I feel so ashamed, Sajidah! I always feel ashamed.'

'But why, Saleema Baji?' She wiped away her tears and looked up at Saleema's flushed face.

'No reason. What does it matter? It's just that ever since I can remember, I've felt ashamed. How nice it would be if I could go mad. Now you go to sleep. Tonight, I have quite a bit of studying to do.'

'And what will happen to my studies, Baji?' Sajidah asked suddenly. She was sure that no one in that house cared about her education.

'I've spoken to Malik. He said to be patient for a while. Right now, he's barely managing to cover the expenses of Kazim's and my education.' The shame on Saleema's face deepened.

Sajidah looked down. She was thinking about how intelligence should not be allowed to die. She'd been brought here to save her intelligence from certain death.

'He's right,' she said, looking up at Saleema.

'You will definitely continue your studies, Sajidah. Kazim's education will be completed in just a year and a half. Then, you can do whatever you want.'

Sajidah stared at her vacantly.

'Are you even listening to what I'm saying?' asked Saleema.

'Yes, Baji . . .' replied Sajidah sadly. She was remembering how her Abba used to repeat the Persian saying: *He who is bitten by a poisonous snake will die before an antidote arrives from Iraq.*

'Now I'm going, you go to sleep.' Saleema hugged her affectionately and left.

One year, two years . . . how many years might pass in the blink of an eye? If only she hadn't come here; if only she'd stayed at the camp. She herself had placed so many obstacles in the way of Salahuddin finding her. He might have looked for her at the camp and then gone away. He might have been too afraid to seek her out publicly from village to village just yet. Who knew if he would make the rounds again?

As she considered this, she decided she would return to the camp the next day. Once she'd made this decision, she was at peace. She dimmed the light and lay down comfortably in her bed.

'Did you already go to sleep, Baji?' asked Taji, knocking softly on the door.

She got up, opened the door, and turned on the light.

'What is it, Taji?'

'Sometimes I'm so tired, I just can't get to sleep, Baji. I got tired of lying in bed, so I came to you.'

She wrapped herself in a scrap of torn blanket and sat down on the floor.

'Do you smoke this hookah, Baji?' she asked. 'Oh, what fun you must have. If you want, I'll fill it up. There's still some fire left in the hearth.' She gazed greedily at the hookah on the shelf.

'This is a memento of my father, Taji,' explained Sajidah with a sigh.

'Oh!'

Taji laid her head on her knees and sighed.

'Taji, how is it that you speak Urdu so well? You're Punjabi, but you only speak in Urdu.'

Taji burst out giggling.

'You're amazed, aren't you, Baji? Girls that work from house to house cleaning learn all different languages. At the zamindar's house where I used to wash dishes, he had three wives. One he'd married and brought from Nukhlow (this was how Taji said 'Lucknow'). She was just like a little doll. Both her co-wives were united against her—no one spoke to her—so when I finished work, I'd sit with her for hours. We were both alone, Baji . . .'

'You have no family at all, Taji?' asked Sajidah.

'First, you tell me, Baji, you're not angry with me, are you? I made a joke, but when you started to cry, swear to God, I started crying too! Saleema Baji couldn't talk back to Kazim Miyan, so she went after me instead.' Taji's voice became tearful. 'It's never the poor person's fault. No one listens to us!' she said, as she wiped away her tears.

'No, no, I've forgotten the whole thing already! I have no quarrel with you. Now tell me, do you have no father, brother, mother? No one at all?'

'No one at all, Baji! I did have a mother, but she is no more.'

'Did she die as well?' Sajidah asked sadly.

'It would have been better if she had. My father died when I was very small. For a year or two, my mother held me to her heart and wept, but then she fell for a man from another community. When our people found out, a Panchayat was called. Do you know, Baji, what they said?' she asked with a deep sigh, looking up at Sajidah innocently.

'What did they say?'

'In front of the whole community they said that love recognizes no caste or clan, the way sleep doesn't notice if the bed is broken . . .' she fell silent.

'Then, Taji?'

'Then what could she do, Baji? She continued to raise me, out of fear of the community, but when I was ten years old, she sent me out to work. I plucked ears of corn alone in the sun during the harvest, I washed dishes at the zamindar's house. I washed their clothing and did all sorts of work. I've worked so hard, Baji. Then the riots started. No one paid attention to community any more. My mother pushed me into a kafila. "Go to your country," she said, "and grab the hand of an honest man." Then she disappeared, grasping the hand of the man who wore a steel bracelet.'

Taji broke down sobbing.

'Don't cry, Taji!' said Sajidah tearfully. She was thinking about how Taji's mother had gone off with the man with the steel bracelet, but now her daughter was finding no honest hand of her own. She was already prostrate with exhaustion at such a young age.

Taji wiped her tears with her dirty palms.

'When the crop ripened, I would get seeds from the zamindar's house, and on those days, my mother was so happy, and she'd go to the bazaar to sell them. I mean to say, Sajidah Baji, if my mother had sold me off to some man the way she sold those seeds . . .' she sighed deeply, and then she plunged her hand into her blouse, looking for something. 'Baji! Let me smoke a bit of cigarette.'

She held up a half-burnt cigarette, lit it, and calmly took a long puff.

'Don't take cigarettes from him any more, Taji,' admonished Sajidah.

'Don't be mad, Baji! When I get a bit dizzy from the smoke, then all my exhaustion goes away. Kazim Miyan is extremely nice. He's the only sympathetic person in this household. Sometimes he secretly gives me quicklime.'

'And you're not ashamed to take it?' she asked, feeling angry with Taji.

'You don't know what everyone is like here, Baji! They're all wretched. No one gives me a single paisa. But Kazim Miyan always says, "When I become an officer, Taji, I'll pay you a salary." See, Baji? He's very nice. Anyway, when will you start going to college like Saleema Baji?' asked Taji, looking at her with sudden disgust.

Sajidah was alarmed by her gaze. 'Very soon, Taji. I'll enrol after a little while.'

Taji laughed hysterically.

'That "little while" will never come, Baji! Saleema Baji's mother is the only one in charge here. Malik is in her clutches, just like my mother was with that man . . .'

Taji suddenly looked terrified. She stubbed out the cigarette with her foot and sat up, clasping her hands before Sajidah.

'They'll murder me. Please don't complain about me to anyone, I beg you.'

'I won't say a word to anyone.'

She grabbed Taji by the shoulders and pulled her up. 'Anyway, I'm going back to the camp tomorrow.'

'What? You're going . . .?' Taji burst out weeping as she walked towards the door. 'Don't go, Baji. Don't go . . .' she said as she left the room.

9

The next morning, while eating breakfast, she gave everyone a cursory glance. They were all eating busily.

'I am leaving today,' she said calmly.

She was confident that no one would care whether she stayed or left, so she was alarmed when she saw that everyone stared back at her questioningly. Nazim put down the teacup he was raising to his lips.

'Where will you go?' asked Saleema, glaring at her.

'To the refugee camp, where I came from. Back there,' she replied quietly.

'Have you gone mad?' Saleema practically screamed. 'You can't go anywhere!' She pounded the table with her fist.

Sajidah was alarmed to see this feisty side of Saleema. All the same, she liked her very much at that moment.

'Did we get this table for free? If you plan to break it, then pick it up and throw it,' cried Saleema's mother angrily.

'Don't get so angry, dear,' Malik admonished softly.

'Do not speak on behalf of my mother—my respected mother—Malik!' Saleema retorted sternly.

Sajidah panicked and stood up. She didn't want things to get worse. And she hadn't expected Saleema to get so emotional at the mere mention of her leaving. She was alarmed that Saleema could talk to her uncle like that, and that he would just smile and put her off.

'You're putting everyone in a bad mood for no good reason,' declared Kazim, rising from his chair and placing a hand on Saleema's shoulder. 'If she leaves, Saleema Baji, we'll go back and get her again. Isn't that right, brother?' he asked, glancing at Nazim mischievously.

'No one can force her to stay,' interrupted Saleema's mother.

'Mother! For God's sake, please don't say anything!' Saleema begged, looking ashamed again. 'You won't go anywhere, Sajidah Baji. You won't have any trouble here!' She grabbed Sajidah's hand and sat her back down in the chair.

'You are alone, and the world is full of evil,' said Nazim's mother, addressing Sajidah for the first time.

'Then, Amma, tell me how to find a world that is full of good.' Sajidah's eyes brimmed with tears.

Nazim's mother looked at her as if to say, *I've forgotten the way to that world.*

'You cannot ignore the words of my Begum, Sajidah Bibi. You will be happy here. You'll get used to it after a while. Isn't that right, Saleema Bibi?' Malik asked Saleema in a beseeching tone.

'Yes, Malik! I won't let her leave,' replied Saleema, her gaze downcast. 'I don't know what happens to me, I just get angry all of a sudden. You forgive me, don't you?'

'For what?' laughed Malik.

'Such a small matter—why is everyone objecting? Sajidah Begum is going nowhere. Isn't that right, dear brother?' asked Kazim.

Nazim did not reply and left the room silently with his head down. Kazim guffawed.

Sajidah wished she could get up and sew Kazim's lips together so that he'd never be able to guffaw in that foul way again.

'I'm going. I'm definitely going,' she declared, pushing back her chair loudly. 'If I must listen to such foul guffawing from Kazim Sahib, I will go mad.'

Kazim stared at her with astonishment and she glared back murderously.

Saleema's mother intervened, her face turning red, 'You're an odd girl! You've pulled your chair out so hard it seems like you want to rip up the floor. I've spent my entire life looking after every single thing in this household, and you have no control over your tongue!'

'Sajidah! Go to your room, I'll talk to you after I get back from college. And you, Kazim Bhai, you will definitely come in first in the CSP exam,' cried out Saleema tearfully.

'You speak sarcastically to your own brother on behalf of this girl who says she wants to get away from you after only two days?' asked Saleema's mother, glancing sharply at Sajidah.

Sajidah rushed off to her room. After that, she had no idea who said what to whom. As she entered her room, she felt as though she was blind, dumb, and deaf; as though her brain had gone into a deep sleep, and now she couldn't think about anything at all. She lay on her bed in that state for a long time. There was a quiet knock on the door, but she didn't hear it. The door opened softly. Nazim entered and leaned against the wall by the door. Sajidah awoke at that moment. She sat up.

'Have you come to point out my accounting error?' she asked, gazing at Nazim vacantly.

'I've come to beg forgiveness for what happened. Anyway, I'm not responsible for all that. The only thing that's my fault, Sajidah Bibi, is that I'm a member of this household, and that's it.' Nazim spoke without looking at her.

'Then, what can I do?' she asked helplessly.

'I did not break the lock on this house, nor did I make you a member of this family, so I've done nothing wrong.'

She turned her face away from Nazim with disgust.

'All I want to say, Sajidah Bibi, is that you aren't going anywhere. You wouldn't even know the way. You would just get lost. But you're not going.'

Nazim left just as quietly as he'd come, without waiting for her response.

Sajidah wished that she could run after him, demanding, 'Who are you? What are you to me? Who has given you the right to stop me?' But instead, she remained frozen on the bed. Once her anger was under control, she thought about the fact that if she were to leave the house, she really wouldn't know the way, and there was no well-wisher to come and guide her. If nothing else, at least Saleema was here . . . Saleema . . .

10

Her conversation with Nazim was long over when she finally decided to live in that house. On the day she made her decision, Sajidah lay silently in her room all through the day and spent the night crying, before finally falling into a deep pit of forbearance. That night, she thought about how deprivation, endurance and captivity all define what it is to be a woman. Once this notion had occurred to her, she tossed and turned. She resolved that she would erase those well-worn and popular definitions of womanhood the way one would errors in a balance sheet. After that day, she decided that she would live in that house as though it was her right. And because of this resolution, everyone in the household had grown friendly towards her, besides Kazim and Saleema's mother, Khala Bi.

Kazim often teased her, 'Great Napoleon! If ever you conquer Khala Bi or me, I will accept your greatness. The others are fools who consider you one of their own and agree with everything you say.'

'You . . .? You are nothing. As for Khala Bi, I have not yet become interested in her,' Sajidah would reply easily, and busy herself with some task as though Kazim were nothing more than a mound of dirt in her path.

'Me? I . . .' he responded, his chest swelling with pride, '. . . I am very important, Sajidah Begum! This you will soon learn.' There was a threatening edge to his tone. For a little while, Sajidah trembled with fear, but then she began to feel herself even stronger than before.

Whenever there was a political row after dinner, she would accompany Nazim's and Kazim's mother, Amma Bi, into her room. She felt as much attachment for Amma Bi as she felt hatred for Nazim. She didn't know why, but she glimpsed in Amma Bi's face the thirsty dove that wanders about in search of water during a heat wave. Nowadays she happened to spend a great deal of time in Amma Bi's room because the MA course was proving difficult for Saleema.

'Do you truly love me, Sajidah?' Amma Bi asked her suddenly one day.

Sajidah panicked at the unexpected question.

'Love . . .?' she asked, steadying herself. 'Whatever you believe, Amma Bi, I find peace with you, and I sense the same fragrance of love from being with you as I did with Abba.' She hung her head helplessly.

An oddly peaceful expression fluttered across Amma Bi's face for a moment.

'You do know that even my own children don't love me,' she remarked, looking about abstractedly.

'How can that be, Amma Bi?'

'Anything is possible. Kazim is very much his father's son. And Nazim, he's grown distant from me because I don't know how to fight for my rights. That foolish boy doesn't understand that one can win much from fighting—but not love.'

Sajidah suddenly remembered what Taji had said: *Saleema's mother is like my mother, Baji!*

'Who has snatched away your love, Amma Bi?' asked Sajidah softly, holding onto Amma Bi's hand, which had grown cold as ice.

'It was never a question of stealing my love. We were engaged when we were still children. When I grew up, I fell in love with my fiancé like every foolish girl, but he was in love with my cousin, Aminah. Do you know who Aminah is? She is Saleema's mother, Khala Bi. But no one knew this then. We got married. Nazim was born. And when Kazim was about to enter this world, Aminah became a widow. Malik brought Aminah and Saleema into our home. I was very happy, and the world praised him for his generosity as well. But then she began to get ideas.'

'Then what happened, Amma Bi?'

'Then what? Then I found out everything. After Aminah arrived, Malik began to drink heavily. I had to sever my ties with him. I began to hate Kazim just because he was being raised by Aminah, and he looked like his father—oh dear!' She rubbed her face. 'The hell of hatred is more horrifying than hell itself. Do you think I'm wrong?'

'No!'

'And Nazim wanted me to get out of that hell. When he became aware of the situation, he insisted that I leave his father, that I divorce him, that I get remarried, and . . .' She suddenly began to sob and then quickly wiped away her tears and sat with her head lowered as though she was ashamed of her feelings. Sajidah could see clearly that she was questioning what Sajidah meant to her—why was she telling her all this?

'Amma Bi, think of me as your daughter. Do you not trust me at all?' Sajidah asked softly, even though she felt embarrassed to ask the question. How could she trust her own voice? This was the same voice that had called out to Allah, the same voice that had muttered curses.

Amma Bi sat quietly thinking, her head down. Sajidah didn't know what to say. She began to wonder if Malik really hadn't had the moral fibre to declare his love before he got married. He had abandoned two lives in the mouth of hell and drowned himself in a sea of liquor. It's so easy to escape from the truth. What a horrid way to make a show of one's love. Had Malik ever given this any thought? Today, for the first time she felt sympathy for Saleema's mother. Did anyone ever consider the situation from her perspective—that this was a physical prison for her, where her desires, thoughts, tears, sighs, all endured punishment for the crime of love?

'Now that you're here, I'm a little less lonely. I've been completely alone for twenty years. Saleema tried hard to befriend me but for some reason I couldn't feel close to her. She's a very good girl. I do know for certain that she loathes her mother.'

Sajidah didn't reply. She suddenly thought of the look of shame on Saleema's face.

When Nazim walked quietly into the room, Sajidah stood up to leave.

'Sit, Sajidah Bi! I'll leave,' he said, gazing at her.

Sajidah left without replying. The moonlight shone through the open window in her room, wafting across her bed. She lay down without turning on the light. She was still thinking about how some of the greatest crimes in this world had been committed in the name of love. Champions of love had caused such sorrow, deprivation and plunder. They had seized everything they could in the name of love, but all the same, people could not stop themselves from loving. Sajidah suddenly began to weep at her audacity, and when she had cried her heart out, she swore to herself that she would never forget Salahuddin; that her waiting would never come to an end.

She got up and stood by the window. In the moonlight, the trees and plants looked hazy, but she could see what looked like two large bundles lying beneath the old leafy peepal tree. She couldn't tell what they were . . . perhaps there were people sitting there. But who could it be? She felt alarmed. A short while later, the two bundles got up and began to walk, and she stood frozen to the spot as they walked past her window. Taji walked towards the garage and Kazim stepped onto the veranda. Then she heard the front door open and close.

Sajidah fell upon her bed. She kept thinking about how Taji's mother had pushed her into the kafila and told her to grab an honest man's hand in her new country. Now how could she make Taji understand that the hand she held was very crooked indeed.

Early the next morning, after she had rolled up her bedding and returned to her room, Sajidah suddenly felt tranquil. The night before, when she'd gone out to the back lawn to sleep, the fragrance of the night-blooming jasmine had made her miss her old home, and she had wept as she'd replied *hmm hmm* to everything Saleema had said. During the past year, she'd come to terms with her situation and found some relief from her memories. Her loneliness and recollections were as prickly as a co-wife, so she tried to keep herself busy at all times.

She quickly walked out of her room and into the hallway where Khala Bi was dusting the vases. Khala Bi went into Kazim's room.

'Just look at the rooms of these three. They're all grown up, but they're so disorderly. Saleema seems to scatter her things all over on purpose, and Kazim . . .' she said, smiling affectionately, 'is like a two-year-old child. Tidying up his room makes me break into a sweat. Nazim is the only one who keeps his room properly.' Khala Bi lovingly tidied Kazim's room as Sajidah stood to one side watching. She thought perhaps she should clean Saleema's and Nazim's rooms herself.

'Your Kazim is not a child. He's the very oldest of all,' she said sarcastically, but Khala Bi didn't pick up on her tone.

'Yes, well, he is extremely wise, the best at his studies. And he's so naughty! He's not unnecessarily serious all the time like Nazim. Because I raised Kazim, didn't I? When he was born, I took him in my arms immediately. Saleema was just two then. Baji never held Kazim for one minute. I didn't have Saleema's milk any more, so I didn't think I'd be able to feed him, but thanks be to Allah, streams of milk began to flow again.

'Yes, I know everything,' retorted Sajidah brusquely.

'What is it that you know?' Khala Bi asked, suddenly startled.

'I know exactly how you raised Kazim. What I'm saying is, if you hadn't been there, this home would be riddled with worms and perhaps Kazim wouldn't have survived,' she said calmly.

'May God give him my life as well. What you are saying is true. If I hadn't been there, this home wouldn't look as it does now. Poor Baji has always been small and thin. And she's always lived apart from everyone else. And well, look, since I'm here, she doesn't have to do any work at all,' she said joyfully.

'Have you people not heard today's news?' asked Nazim, entering the room quietly.

They were both surprised to see him come into Kazim's room.

'Quaid-e-Azam Muhammad Ali Jinnah has passed away,' he announced in a low voice and left the room.

Sajidah felt as though Quaid-e-Azam's body lay in her heart, and she couldn't even cry.

'Oh no! What will happen now!' cried Khala Bi as she went running into the hallway. Sajidah followed her out. 'My goodness, we're not fated to live peacefully! Oh, oh, have you heard? Quaid-e-Azam has died, Malik! Where are you?' she shrieked and then fell to weeping.

Khala Bi's screams alarmed everyone. Amma Bi appeared in her doorway for a moment, and then disappeared again. Taji stood beside Kazim, clutching her heart with dough-smeared hands. Sajidah had not seen Kazim appear.

'Kazim Miyan! What will happen now? I won't go back to my mother,' sobbed Taji.

'Idiot! You're not going anywhere,' said Nazim, glaring at her. Then he closed his eyes. He sat silently, sprawled on the chair in the hallway.

'Well, now we'll lose this home. Prepare to go into your quarters. Now that scoundrel won't let us live in peace!' Some time ago, Malik had begun drinking in the morning. He was now stumbling about.

'Which scoundrel is that?'

'Him—him—your old man, the one whose house you're in!' screamed Malik.

Nazim turned his face away in disgust.

'Go back to your room, Malik!' said Khala Bi, as she led him away.

Just then Saleema arrived. Her eyes were red. Schools, colleges, offices—everything had been closed.

'You've also been crying, Saleema Bi! I've seen people beating their heads against walls in back lanes, weeping,' said Nazim, but Saleema didn't reply.

'What will happen now, Bhai Miyan?' Kazim asked. Today, for the first time, he looked frightened. Sajidah felt oddly peaceful at that moment.

'Yes! Now what will happen?' Nazim looked at Kazim with disgust. 'How strange it is that with Quaid-e-Azam's demise countless people imagine the death and destruction of this country. Why doesn't anyone consider that the existence of this country is the outcome of the struggle of many? They've forgotten their own existences with the death of just one leader. Grief in its place, but is this not the ill-fate of our country?'

Nazim suddenly got up, opened the front door, and went out.

Sajidah was about to go to her room when she saw that Taji still stood behind the door weeping. Sajidah put an affectionate hand on her shoulder.

'Don't cry, Taji! Nothing will happen, nothing at all. You will stay here, in Pakistan. You'll never have to go back to your mother.'

Taji said nothing. She walked away slowly, her head down. Sajidah sat down on her bed. Today, for the first time she'd liked what Nazim had to say, and it had calmed her. And then suddenly, she remembered Gamo. *Drink tea hot-hot! Eat naan, soft-soft!* Who could dare harm a country where such people lived?

11

Nazim had resigned from the Department of Rehabilitation
and was teaching at a college now. Sometimes he came home
from college to eat lunch, but mostly he was away. When
he returned at night, he'd have a few friends with him, and
Taji would have to make them cup after cup of tea, cursing
them all the while. This routine upset Kazim and Malik. The
conversations about politics had stopped. Now, even ~~Saleema~~
rarely had a chance to talk with Nazim. But Sajidah was happy
to escape from all the chattering.

It was starting to get extremely cold. After dinner, she
went into Saleema's room and was astonished to see that
Saleema, who studied quietly every evening, lay face down on
her bed sobbing.

'Saleema Baji,' Sajidah called out softly. 'What's wrong?'

'Nothing, Sajjo, nothing . . .' Saleema wrapped herself
in her quilt and sat up. 'You come sit by me too,' she said,
holding one end of the quilt out to Sajidah.

Sajidah sat down and covered her feet with the quilt.

'Now tell me this, why were you crying?' she asked.

'No reason. Sometimes I just want to cry my heart out,
and if I don't cry, I feel as though my heart will burst.'

'But why, Baji? Everything must have a reason.'

'There are some things you're scared to admit even to yourself. You run from them your whole life, and . . .'

'. . . all the same they stick to you like a shadow,' Sajidah added in a hollow tone. She began to think about how shadows dissolve as soon as the sun goes down; but what are these shadows on which the sun never sets?

'What were you just thinking about?' asked Saleema.

Sajidah smiled and looked at her. It was clear from her face that she was making a conscious effort to change the subject.

'Saleema Baji, are you fond of Nazim Sahib?' asked Sajidah.

She did not expect Saleema's reaction to be so violent; she stared at Sajidah with such shock and disgust, it made her shudder, and she continued to stare at her until she burst into tears of shame.

'I cannot even imagine having a man in my life. For me, the eternal bond between man and woman has no meaning. That's why the question of being fond or not doesn't arise, understand, Sajidah Bibi?' said Saleema, placing a hand on Sajidah's shoulder.

Saleema looked down and suddenly seemed completely fine. Now, only those traces of shame remained on her face that had become a regular part of her features.

'I'm extremely embarrassed, Sajjo!' she said. 'Come, dry your tears now, forgive me.'

'You're trying to make me even more embarrassed,' replied Sajidah, standing up. 'Please forgive me.'

She hurried out of the room and returned to her own, where she sat in solitude thinking of Saleema who had refused the eternal bond between man and woman. But why? And now she could think of nothing else when Taji came and sat down on the floor in her distinctive fashion.

'Why are you growing so weak, Taji?' asked Sajidah, looking at her carefully. Taji's round cheeks looked withered and under the weak electric light her skin had a sallow cast.

'I work so hard, Baji! So much that if you . . .' She fell silent for a moment. 'Well, if only my luck would turn! They say that after twelve years even a horse's luck will turn, and I'm human, after all.' She sighed deeply.

'You're the very best human. Your luck will surely change, Taji.'

'Oh, oh! Now I must go,' Taji cried out. She got up and headed swiftly towards the door as though she'd just recalled some very important chore.

Now Sajidah was sad and alone again. With great effort, she managed to turn her attention away from Saleema and pick up the books lying on the teapoy. Ever since she'd enrolled in college, she'd started staying up late at night, studying, but today she couldn't read one word. She began to wonder if Nazim was trying to put her in his debt by taking responsibility for her college expenses, or if he was just fulfilling his duty. After all, he had taken her away from the camp. Well, she didn't believe in indebtedness and all that anyway. Once she was independent, she'd pay him back every penny.

But she simply couldn't study at that moment. She put the books back on the teapoy, feeling exhausted. Night loomed before her like a mountain. She could neither study nor sleep. *I wonder what Saleema must be doing right now*, she thought.

When she got up to lock the door, she could hear Malik bellowing in the hallway. She heard this every night, along with Khala Bi's soft sobbing. But just as she was locking the door, Taji returned. *Oh, good*, Sajidah thought. *Now I can pass some time.*

Taji lit a cigarette the moment she sat down and began to inhale deeply.

'I had two annas. I got these from the bazaar, Baji,' explained Taji, clearly lying.

When Sajidah looked at her closely, Taji became nervous and shrank into her blanket.

'Taji!' said Sajidah, gazing at her reproachfully.

'Why are you staring at me like that, Baji?' Taji asked, suddenly looking quite innocent.

'I like you very much, Taji! I want you always to be happy. Once I've made something of myself, I'll arrange for you to marry an honest man. There will be drums and fanfare on that day! But, Taji, the hand you're holding onto right now is very bad and . . .'

'Look, Baji!' snapped Taji, turning red with rage. 'Don't interfere with my business. Did I ever interfere with yours? Have I ever asked why Nazim pays for your education?' she asked, glancing at her sharply.

Sajidah felt angry but she managed to control herself. Really, how could she make Taji understand? She pitied her.

'Time to go, Taji. Time for you to go to sleep. I'm feeling tired.'

'You won't complain about me to Saleema Baji, will you? I was rude to you,' said Taji, gazing at her fearfully.

'No, I won't, but now you go away.'

Taji left quietly. Sajidah closed the door and lay down, covering her face with the quilt. Taji also had the right to say what she was thinking, after all. But what she said would reflect her limited perspective. Sajidah lay thinking a long while that night.

12

That night, a fierce argument took place at the dinner table. The issue was simply this: Khala Bi's tears had been so effective that Malik had been keeping perfectly sober from morning until nine or ten at night for some time now. And this perfect sobriety was now emerging in full colour today. Somehow, he'd gotten the idea that Nazim had caused irreparable harm to the household by leaving his employment at the Department of Rehabilitation, and now he insisted on knowing his reasons for leaving the job. All Nazim did was sit and eat his dinner silently.

'I know you don't want to talk to anyone in this house. You've been staying out all day for quite a while and you've been behaving oddly, but today I'm asking once and for all, why are you trying to destroy this household? Why are you stealing my legal rights?' thundered Malik.

'All right, I'll tell you why,' retorted Nazim. 'I quit that job because there was such corruption, such dishonesty, such bribery, such vileness, that if I'd stayed there, I would have gone mad.'

'I'll tell you what it is, dear brother!' interjected Kazim. 'You don't have what it takes to stay in a job like that. Also, you didn't want us to get the orchard and the second mansion either.'

'Why don't you try your luck then, Kazim. Maybe you can get a job there,' suggested Saleema sarcastically.

'I wouldn't work at such a low job. You wait and see what happens when I pass the competitive exam,' announced Kazim proudly.

'Yes, we know what you'll do; exactly what all those other people are doing, or a bit more. But remember that you people will not be able to support this administration for long,' replied Nazim calmly.

'Why don't you say what you're thinking?' asked Sajidah. 'All this debating secretly at home . . .'

'Why? Why say it out in the open? Who are you to egg them on?' snapped Khala Bi.

Sajidah began tapping her finger quietly by her plate as though she hadn't heard anything.

'So many safety acts and ordinances have been established to censor people that if you stand in the street and talk loudly, the government will accuse you of sloganeering and arrest you. I have no desire to go to jail. In jail, a man becomes completely helpless, and I don't have the courage of a Gandhi,' said Nazim.

'If you turn into a Gandhi, then a Godse will shoot you,' chuckled Kazim loudly.

'Kazim! Are you laughing? The murder of Gandhi is a chapter in history that will be forever drenched in tears,' cried Saleema, gazing at him with disgust.

'Amazing! So, you too have begun speaking out,' retorted Kazim, returning her look and then laughing loudly. 'My dear brother, when you take your magic outside the house, you must be poisoning the minds of your students! Although you look about as innocent as a laughing Buddha. But I know you, you're against Pakistan in your heart,' added Kazim turning serious.

'Every critic is called a traitor nowadays.'

'Then come out in the open!' cried Kazim excitedly.

'For the time being, my work is teaching children.'

'For God's sake, Nazim! Stop this garbage! I'm fed up with everyone's politicking. I have no connection with the world. I just want to live life peacefully,' said Malik, looking exceptionally revolted.

'You've always lived your life in peace, Malik,' retorted Nazim. 'You've always remained oblivious to what goes on around you. Your world is limited to what you see around you, and that's it. You act just like the rulers of Pakistan, and . . .'

'Enough! Enough, Nazim! Have you no shame criticizing your father? You're talking nonsense. There's a limit to shamelessness,' scolded Khala Bi, turning pink with rage.

'Don't say anything to him, Khala Bi,' said Kazim. 'The poor man is clueless. He doesn't know anything about Muslim victories. He's forgetting what happened yesterday. He doesn't even remember the victory in Kashmir.'

'Oh, I had forgotten—are you speaking of the Kashmir which is still three-quarters in India?' asked Nazim softly. Then suddenly he screamed, 'You're ignorant, Kazim! As long as I'm here, you've got to leave the room.'

'*Get out*,' Kazim said, mimicking him. 'Actually, I'm the one that broke the lock on this house; you don't even have

it in you. This house is mine. *You* get out of here!' he cried,
enraged.

Nazim pushed his chair back loudly and left the room.
For a little while, all was silent. Saleema stared at the door in
astonishment. Then, she suddenly turned around and began
screaming at the top of her lungs.

'You, Kazim! You're shameless! You're vile! There's no
limit to how low you'll go. If you can learn nothing from
your brother, at least keep a civil tongue in your head. My
mother didn't raise you well, otherwise you'd be able to speak
properly to civilized people. And you, Malik, you've nurtured
this insolent . . .'

'Enough, enough, Saleema Baji! I respect you, don't get
me started on you. You should know that if Malik hadn't
adopted you, you'd now . . .'

'Shut up, you cheeky devil!' yelled Malik. But then his
anger subsided. 'I won't stop anyone. I got absolutely nothing
at all by coming to Pakistan. All I got was this abuse. May
God not make this any father's fate,' he fretted.

Amma Bi, who had been silently eating, got up and went
to her room.

'And you, Malik, don't be so sad. May your enemies weep,'
cried Khala Bi, bursting into tears. She began crying like a baby.
She looked distressed, like someone who'd just been robbed.

Kazim quietly got up and left. Saleema sat ripping a piece
of roti into smaller and smaller bits and dropping them onto
her plate. And Sajidah stared in astonishment at Khala Bi's
face, which seemed to reflect Malik's sorrows.

Malik sighed quietly, leaning his head back in his large
chair, his eyes closed.

'Come, Malik. Come to your room and rest. Don't take the children's words so seriously,' said Khala Bi, placing a hand on his shoulder. 'Go on, why are you two girls sitting there and staring at me?'

'I don't know who's right or wrong,' Saleema's voice dropped to a whisper as they walked down the hallway. 'It was so much better than this, before the Partition, when we lived in three-room government quarters. Even if we knew everything, no one opened their mouths, no one talked loudly for fear of the family and the neighbours. Kazim would tease me, goad me, and say all sorts of strange things, but I said not one word to him. I was frightened to speak, but here there are no neighbours, nor members of the family . . .' She sighed deeply and fell silent, then went into her room.

'All right then, goodnight, Sajjo. Who knows where Nazim Bhai must have gone. Go to sleep. It's quite late.'

Saleema locked her door from the inside and Sajidah walked to her own room with tired feet.

13

In those days, Sajidah had started noticing a familiar face
at college. Often, when she came out of class at lunchtime
and sat beneath the old peepal tree, a girl she recognized
passed by in a small group. Sajidah wished she could talk
with her, but she didn't have the courage. What if she
wasn't Anwari? How beautifully styled and trimmed her
hair was, and she wore expensive clothing. She'd studied
with her up to class eight, but then Anwari had left school.
Back then, her clothing had been cheap and shabby, and
she had worn her hair so tightly braided it looked like a
tail curving down her back. Anwari's father, Kaloo Baba,
used to work as the water man, delivering water to the
entire *mohalla*. Two water bags per anna. He wore a thick
red cloth covering his face like a veil, and whenever he
visited Sajidah's house, she was sure to ask after Anwari.
Kaloo Baba would reply proudly, 'I've put her in purdah,
daughter. Let the community joke if they wish. She was
turning too many heads and getting whistled at. She'll take
the class ten exam privately now. I just love that she studies
so much. I walk about the community with my head held
high . . .'

'And she'll keep studying, Baba! Anwari is very bright,' Sajidah would say, and Baba would laugh inside his red veil and then go on his way.

One day, when that familiar looking girl passed by alone as though looking for something, Sajidah got up and walked up behind her. She placed a hand on her shoulder, and the girl turned around.

'You're Anwari, aren't you? I'm Sajidah, remember?' asked Sajidah looking at her affectionately.

Anwari blanched. She looked anxious, as though she'd been caught red-handed committing a sin. It was clear from her eyes that she wanted to set fire to Sajidah's trove of memories and flee.

'Yes, that's . . . me . . . I . . .' Anwari couldn't seem to finish her sentence.

'Oh, no need to be frightened. You don't recognize me— I'm Sajidah. How is Kaloo Baba? What class are you studying in here?'

She'd noticed the large mole on Anwari's hand, which, in the old days, she used to press when she tried to get Anwari to agree with her.

'Father is well. He works at a store here. And Baji, there's also a fabric mill. Abba worked very hard. We've built a nice big house too, and Baji . . .'

'How splendid, Anwari! Well, you're looking really lovely, but you don't seem happy to see me. You're rich now, aren't you?'

'No, Baji, I'm afraid. No one here knows that I'm the daughter of a waterman. Here, everyone thinks I'm the daughter of a mill owner. Abba has even changed his name, Baji. Now he is Saroor Hussein. You won't tell anyone, will you, Baji?' she asked, staring at her entreatingly.

'Rest assured, I won't tell anyone a thing.'

Sajidah let go of Anwari's hand that she'd held so fondly.

'May nothing else interfere with the natural course of your life, Anwari,' said Sajidah, determining in her heart of hearts that she would not attempt to speak with her again.

'Baji! You were offended. Please understand; Abba's back was doubled over from carrying sacks of water. When Allah created Pakistan, our luck changed. No one knows one another here. Some of our community is in Karachi, the rest in Delhi. Some were murdered. Now there's no one left to remember Kaloo Baba the water carrier. He has scores of employees now,' she added with pride.

Anwari's friends were walking towards her. She ran back to them.

14

It had been eleven or twelve days since Nazim had left home.
Everyone was upset. Khala Bi rushed about anxiously. Saleema
sat with her books in front of her, staring into space. Amma
Bi hardly touched her food. Malik seemed to have entirely
forgotten about his orchard and mansion. Only Kazim was
cheerful. He teased everyone and scolded Saleema constantly.
Since Nazim had left, Sajidah had noticed that Kazim had
started to stare at her insolently. She kept thinking about how
Nazim's presence was necessary to keep the household under
control, although she did not miss him. To this day, she had
not managed to overcome her initial hatred for Nazim.

At the dinner table that night, Saleema started an uproar.

'Go, why don't you? Go look for Nazim Bhai and find out
where he is. You just sit there cheerfully eating your meals,
stuffing the food in all the way up to your neck,' she said to
Kazim, glaring at him as though she wanted to murder him.

'Shall I put out a missing person advertisement, Saleema
Baji?' he asked with a chortle.

'I . . . I'll break your head, Kazim!' Saleema cried, beside
herself with rage. Everyone looked at her with surprise and
alarm.

Now Kazim, too, had turned red with boiling rage. 'You wouldn't be able to break one of my fingers, let alone my head, Saleema Baji! I respect you, but that doesn't mean you can treat me like a . . .'

Malik stopped eating and went off to his room. Ever since Nazim had left, he'd begun to drink in the early evening again. Intoxication turns men into cowards and it also makes them forget who they are. It destroys their ability to see reason.

'You're so vulgar! So crude! If ever I didn't do right by you in your life, I'll change my name,' screamed Saleema.

'Then you go ahead and change your name as quickly as you can, because you're nothing!' cried Kazim, standing up and pushing his chair back noisily.

Khala Bi had sat silently until now, as though the faculty of speech had been snatched from her. She raised both her hands with great effort and placed them on her head.

'You can all go ahead and kill me, take revenge on me, take revenge on me . . . on me.' She burst out weeping.

'I hate you! I hate you!' screamed Saleema, spitting on the floor.

'Please get out of here, Saleema Baji. Get up,' urged Sajidah.

She pulled Saleema up from her chair and made her stand.

'Don't you interfere, you munshi spawn!' roared Kazim.

'Oh, is that all you can come up with?' Sajidah laughed. 'At least I'm the daughter of a man who kept his books true, and I'm proud of my father, but you have nothing at all to be proud of.'

'You're attacking my father!' yelled Kazim, leaping towards Sajidah.

Amma Bi, who until now had sat quietly listening to them all, rose and grabbed Kazim by the collar.

'You'd raise your hand against a sister?'

'Oh, I'll show her, I'll show her!'

Sajidah dragged Saleema off to her room. Kazim kept on screaming. She laid Saleema down on her bed and locked the door from the inside.

Saleema was sobbing.

'Quiet, quiet, Baji. There's no use weeping over the words of that madman!'

'He's not a madman, Sajjo. You have no idea how much pain he's caused me! Who knows where Nazim must be now. He must be having such a hard time surviving. He took part in the Pakistan movement night and day. Kazim, Malik and my mother were always accusing him of participating in the movement so that he could make those with homes homeless. And now they're looting Pakistan and filling their bellies and can't tolerate a single word of criticism from us,' cried Saleema with rage.

'Go to sleep now, Baji. Just forget everything,' said Sajidah, placing her hands lovingly on Saleema's swollen eyes. 'Go to sleep, Baji!'

When Saleema turned over and closed her eyes, Sajidah went to her own room. Taji was sitting there with her head bowed.

'You've come, Sajidah Baji! I've been sitting here for so long waiting for you. Today, I didn't even wash the dishes. I just took them off the table and piled them up.' Her face was distorted with anger.

'What happened?' asked Sajidah sternly. She was displeased by Taji's presence.

'For one thing, so much work to do; on top of that, the constant fighting. The only person in this house that laughs and talks is Kazim Miyan. And neither you nor Saleema Baji like him. Please don't side with Saleema Baji, Sajidah Baji!'

'Don't talk rubbish, I'm sleepy, go away from here.'

'Go to sleep, who am I to sit here and keep you awake . . .' Taji muttered as she left the room.

When Sajidah got up to lock the door, she could hear Khala Bi talking loudly, her voice awash with joy.

'Where were you, Nazim? Did you ever spare a thought for my feelings? Or what would happen to Saleema? She only talks to you in this house, the rest of us are all . . .'

'Where is Saleema?' asked Nazim.

'She must be in her room.'

Sajidah locked her door, feeling oddly relieved. Outside, the clouds had been gathering since evening, and now suddenly, it began to thunder. Winter was departing, but a touch of chill had returned to the air. A cold breeze blew in through the window. When Sajidah rose to shut the window, she saw two shadows outside walking towards the veranda and felt her heart sink. *It won't be long,* she thought, *till Taji's shadow walks alone. The other shadow will disappear, never to be found again.* Taji was now walking to her quarters in the garage, and Sajidah heard the front door closing.

She shut the window and lay down. She'd only just thought of reading when someone knocked softly on her door. She thought it was Taji; she'd been complaining about not getting enough sleep lately.

When she opened the door, she was alarmed to find Nazim standing there.

'Sajidah Bi, you're all right, aren't you? I'm sorry everyone was disturbed on my account,' said Nazim quietly. 'And Saleema is only close to me in this family. When she saw me, she cried a great deal.'

'But I'm not close to you. There's no need to worry about me,' replied Sajidah calmly.

'That's fine. All the same, it was my duty to ask after you, since I've been gone so long. I brought you to this house, so it's my responsibility to ensure you never have any trouble.'

'The day I came here . . .' she stopped for a moment and looked at Nazim. 'It was an ill-starred moment, Nazim Sahib!' she said tearfully.

There was a loud clap of thunder. If there was anything Sajidah feared, it was thunder. Nazim stared at her for a moment and then left. Sajidah locked the door and lay down on her bed, hiding her face under the quilt to protect herself from the crashing thunder and lightning.

15

For the past nine or ten days, Taji's health had been so bad that she hadn't come out of her quarters. Sajidah went to visit her many times. She checked her pulse and placed her hand on her forehead, but she had neither fever nor cold. All the same, she was growing so thin that her cheekbones jutted out. Khala Bi still hadn't brought a doctor to see her. Instead, she concocted all sorts of nonsense potions to feed her. Sajidah couldn't help but wonder why this woman was going to so much trouble to save a few rupees. Khala Bi had even taken over all responsibilities in the kitchen.

That day, when the maid was done with the housework, Khala Bi had taken her to her bedroom. Sajidah looked on with surprise. Khali Bi considered the maid low-born; she wouldn't even talk to her directly.

'Saleema Baji! Khala Bi has become very progressive today,' said Sajidah, laughing as she peered into her room.

'How's that, Sajjo?'

'She's taken the maid into her room and she's talking to her.'

'Perhaps she's looking for a maulvi?' suggested Saleema, pursing her lips with hatred. 'She must be asking her if she works in the home of a maulvi, and if she does, she'll ask her to bring him over. Then, she'll have another *taweez* written up for Malik so he'll quit drinking and live for all eternity . . .'

Sajidah began to feel pity for Khala Bi. Cowards who make bad decisions in the family are sometimes responsible for great tragedies. They start enormous fires but don't smell the stench of burning. And then everything turns to ash.

'Saleema Baji, how long has Taji been ill? Poor Khala Bi has been cooking every day. Come, today we should cook too. Let's spend our day off doing a good deed.'

'Absolutely not. We'll use too much ghee and we'll throw out the chaff without properly sifting the flour. Malik's carefully saved earnings cannot be wasted like that. Go do some other good deed and leave me to finish my novel—it's very interesting.'

❦

Khala Bi started kicking up a fuss early that evening, insisting that everyone eat early.

'The clouds are gathering,' she warned. 'It might rain!'

Despite everyone refusing to do so, she set the plates out on the table and started to call them to dinner so they were forced to sit down and eat. Sajidah prepared Amma Bi's plate and took it to her bedroom. She'd stopped eating with everyone after Kazim and Nazim had quarrelled.

As Sajidah sat down comfortably in her chair, she cast a glance at everyone else. Khala Bi looked exhausted, and Kazim looked worried for some reason. His face was flushed. Nazim looked exactly the same as always—disconnected from everyone else. If anyone spoke to him, he grunted and put them off. It had been a long time since he'd seemed upset at the dinner table. Kazim could tease all he wanted, but Nazim and Saleema did not respond.

'You, my love, why are you so quiet today? You've always been the one to laugh and play like a child. Why are you so worried?' asked Khala Bi, picking out nice cuts of meat and placing them on Kazim's plate.

'Studying has made my son weak,' lamented Malik, looking at his beloved Kazim. He'd had a few drinks before dinner, so his face was wreathed with smiles.

'It's so cloudy and the wind is moaning—that makes people depressed. The weather influences people, doesn't it? That's why it's better if our mother doesn't get too worried,' remarked Saleema so sarcastically that Khala Bi dropped the food she was eating and started to laugh for no reason.

Kazim glanced at Saleema and then began to eat apathetically.

'All right, everyone eat quickly! If it starts to rain, it'll get colder, and then it's hard to wash the dishes.'

She began to gulp down her food. Kazim was obediently following her orders. Was it really about to turn bitterly cold? Sajidah wasn't even wearing a sweater. Perhaps she was thick-skinned and that's why she wasn't feeling the chill. Everyone was eating quickly, besides Saleema and Nazim. Kazim was the first to finish his meal, after which he left the room. They were soon done with their dinner, except Saleema; she, on the other hand, was eating in a leisurely fashion, taking small bites.

'Saleema, dear, do eat a bit more quickly, I told you . . .' Khala Bi implored, her voice trailing off.

'If you're in such a big hurry, then I'm not eating,' snapped Saleema. She jumped up and left the room.

'It's not like I told anyone to stop eating,' said Khala Bi, her voice tearful. 'She misunderstands everything I say.'

She started clearing the plates quickly.

'Wait . . . I think it's starting to drizzle. There's a sweet fragrance rising in the air. May God protect my children from the cold! This sort of end of winter chill is very dangerous.'

'The cold seems to be extra perilous today,' remarked Nazim softly, but Khala Bi was leaving the room, carrying stacks of plates. Nazim stared at Sajidah, and she suddenly felt nervous. She wondered if the weather truly was dangerous. She went off to Saleema's room and sighed with relief.

After Khala Bi had put the dishes away and returned, she was furious to see that Nazim and Sajidah were sitting in Saleema's room and that Saleema was delivering a commentary on the day's rain.

'I told you all to go sit in your own rooms and wrap yourselves up,' said Khala Bi from the doorway. 'Do you people have so little respect for me that you just make fun of what I say?'

'Enough, Khala Bi! We're all getting ready to sleep. We just happened to sit down for a couple of minutes. It truly is getting cold today,' replied Nazim mildly. He stood up.

'And yes, Nazim, my darling, don't go out to shut the gate, the wind is bitterly cold. I'll shut it myself.'

'Thank you, Khala Bi. Goodnight, Saleema.'

Nazim left for his room. As Sajidah walked towards the door there was a loud clap of thunder.

'Sajidah! Do close the window in your room and draw the curtains tightly. It's so frightening when lightning flashes,' warned Khala Bi.

Sajidah drew her curtains but she didn't turn off the light. There was something odd about Khala Bi's many instructions today. There'd been thunder the night before as well, with great flashes of lightning, but Khala Bi hadn't been worried at all. She picked up a book and tried to forget Khala Bi's peculiar attentions but ended up nodding off. Her eyes fluttered open again and again with the claps of thunder. At some point, sleep abandoned her, and she grew exhausted with tossing and turning. The window was shut, and it was growing humid.

She got up and opened a window panel. What she saw when she peered outside astonished her. The clock was striking one, and Khala Bi was locking the gate and walking towards the garage. She was overwhelmed with terror. Was Taji's condition worsening? Khala Bi must surely have gone to her; perhaps she'd been sitting by her since finishing the housework. She wouldn't call the doctor for fear of the cost, but she was willing to ruin her own health staying up all night. How strange humans are. There are so many layers in their personalities, one grows exhausted peeling them back; even then one rarely gets to the core.

In the morning, after Sajidah awoke, she went to see Taji before even washing her face and hands. Taji looked like she'd been sick for years, like she'd passed through the valley of death the night before. Her eyelids were swollen, her lips chapped, and her quarters stank as though they'd been sprinkled with fresh blood.

'Taji!' Sajidah called out, placing her hand on her forehead. It felt cold as ice..

Taji opened her eyes and peered at Sajidah with great effort.

'I'm all right, Baji,' she answered faintly.

'Oh yes, you're absolutely fine! I had no idea you were this ill,' said Sajidah, stroking her forehead. 'If I'd known, I would have spent the night by your side.'

Taji gazed up at the ceiling with pleading eyes. Tears flowed down her sallow cheeks. She closed her eyes and pulled the filthy quilt over her face.

'Taji, shall I massage your head?' asked Sajidah, pulling the quilt from her eyes, but Taji neither opened her eyes nor spoke. Sajidah stood for a while and then left. She had to get ready for school.

෴

Ten or fifteen days later, Taji was better and back to doing the housework, but she'd lost her playful spirit. Her round face now wore a lost look. Sajidah began to like her more because of this, but now even if she had free time, Taji didn't come to sit with her. One day, as she sat bent over her course books, Taji suddenly burst in. She sat down on the ground, sprawled out in her peculiar way, lit a cigarette butt, and began to smoke furiously.

Sajidah put her books aside.

'You're completely well now, Taji! Your face looks pink again. But where have you been all these days, and why haven't you come to see me?'

'It's nothing, Baji. I just have so much work and no time at all.'

'That day you were so ill, I thought your time was up,' laughed Sajidah.

Taji grinned too.

'Taji, tell me this, why did your quarters smell of blood that day? Did Khala Bi sacrifice a black chicken for you?'

'Baji, that would have been expensive. I was the sacrifice. That's what the smell was.'

She stubbed out her cigarette, got up and left, fighting back her tears.

For a long while, Sajidah regretted making Taji sad for no reason.

16

Sajidah spent the long summer afternoons sitting and chatting with Saleema. They mostly talked of the past, both recent and distant. Strangely, despite her love for Saleema, Sajidah was never able to bring up that part of her past that included Salahuddin; that part of the past she continued to await in her future. She worried someone might wipe out her past with some argument or make her doubt her waiting. At times, when she discussed the subject of love with Saleema, she'd wax serious. Saleema wasn't prepared to change her mind and acknowledge that love between a man and woman was anything besides a kind of hunger, a self-serving hunger that consumes all other bonds and relationships. In her view, the belly of love was never sated.

Sajidah could tell that Saleema's beliefs were reflections of her past, a past that had cast an injurious shadow on her life. And she pitied her. Would she always live deprived of love? But when she tried to make her see reason, Saleema laughed as though, unlike her, Sajidah was just a foolish girl incapable of knowing about any subject in depth. And the tone of her laughter was intolerable.

One night, Sajidah was sitting in Amma Bi's room, chatting, when Nazim came in. When he saw her sitting there, he grew unnecessarily serious.

'And how are you doing, Amma Bi?' he asked in a formal tone.

'And how is your Pakistan? Everything is well, I hope?' replied Amma Bi perfunctorily.

'*My* Pakistan!' he burst out laughing. 'Is it not your Pakistan as well? You people seem to think that Pakistan is just mine. My goal was simply to create such a place. Whatever came of that belongs to all of you.'

'No, not to me. I own nothing whatsoever. Whatever I have belongs to your father, your brother and your Khala Bi. Well, anyway, do tell me, what brings you here to ask after your mother?' she replied sarcastically.

'You are in my heart at all times, Amma Bi,' he said with some embarrassment. 'The thing is, Amma, though you've always lived in a prison of your fancy for the sake of our father, I mean Malik, you must remember that I spent the first few years of my life in your arms. I wasn't raised by Khala Bi like Kazim. I was always hungry for your love, but you . . .'

'Are you telling all this to Sajidah? I've already told her everything; what's left to tell?'

Nazim looked at his mother sadly and left the room with his head down.

'Amma Bi, can I ask you something?' asked Sajidah softly.

'Ask away, but don't let it be about my life. Sajjo, have you ever seen a wounded monkey?'

'Yes, Amma Bi! A wounded monkey once ended up at the house where I used to live. After that, it seemed as though all the monkeys of the city gathered around. They came and picked at its wound and examined it, and then went away. The wound kept growing, and finally one day . . .' Sajidah fell silent.

'. . . and I don't want to die like a wounded monkey,' finished Amma Bi.

After that, the two of them sat in silence for some time. Amma Bi picked up the ladies' magazine from the head of her bed and began to read it carefully, and Sajidah sat there embarrassed, looking about, then tiptoed out of the room and into the hallway. At that moment, she felt quite confused. She wondered if no other emotion existed between love and hate, and if it did, what should it be called?

She hesitated as she passed by Saleema's room and stood still. She could hear Saleema speaking in a deeply pained tone, 'Stay away from them—don't reveal any connections you have with them! If you get caught, then truly I will die. Nazim, my brother, I'm only living in this house for your sake. I could be living independently now. I could go away from here.'

'Saleema, you are my pride! It seems strange to see you crying. Listen, once Confucius was going from district to district with his pupils. Along the way, they encountered a weeping woman. He asked her why she was crying. The woman told him that a tiger had eaten her father-in-law and her children. "Then why do you stay here?" Confucius asked. "Because the government here is not ruled by a tyrant," said the woman. And so, Confucius said to his pupils, "Write this down: A despotic government is more lethal than a tiger."'

For a little while there was complete silence.

'But Nazim, my brother!' Saleema's voice was tearful. 'What can you do?'

Sajidah kept walking. As she entered her room, she wondered if a man who causes errors in the accounting of others could become a leader. Would he be capable of clashing with a despotic government? Memories of Abba broke through her thoughts, and she sat silently for a long while, mourning his death in her heart.

17

It had been cloudy and drizzling all day long, but that night, after she locked her door and tried to sleep, the rain poured down in buckets, as though great holes had been bored into the sky. She noticed a thin stream of water creeping down the wall and remembered a time long ago when it had rained just like this. The gali had filled with water up to her knees, and children splashed about making a racket. A thin stream flowed down the wall from one corner of the ceiling of their new home and it soon began to gush like an open faucet. She'd been terrified that the roof of their house, built on the foundations of a lifetime of Abba's labour, would collapse. She wished she could go up to the roof and shut off the water. Just as she rose to go upstairs, Salahuddin had arrived, his trousers rolled. When he saw the water, he rushed up to the roof, and was back in a short while after patching the hole. She was speechless with gratitude. He was completely soaked from head to toe and washed clean as the jasmine plant.

'I was sure the deluge would come today, and I would drown,' she had said.

'But we haven't sinned!' he said, laughing heartily.

Ↄ

Someone knocked softly on the door.

'Who is it?' asked Sajidah, getting up. *It must be Taji*, she thought. *It's raining so hard, the poor thing must be afraid alone in her quarters.*

But when she opened the door, it was Kazim who came rushing in.

'I thought you might be frightened,' he said, locking the door from the inside.

Sajidah stared at him hard. His eyes radiated hunger. She felt besieged by the storm.

'Kazim! This is not Taji's quarters! Get out of my room. You've come to the wrong place,' she cried, trembling with rage.

'Taji is so much better than you. She eats our salt and repays the debt. You're dependent on us, and here you are, telling me to get out of your room. You're nothing, you're only good for one thing, understand, munshi spawn?' he taunted.

Sajidah felt as though she'd gone mad. She jumped forward, grabbed Kazim by the collar and pushed him so hard, his head hit the wall.

'And this is what you're good for!' she screamed.

Before Kazim could regain his balance, she unlocked the door and ran down the darkened hallway towards Saleema's room. Suddenly, someone placed their hands gently on her shoulders.

'Come into my room, Sajidah Bibi! Don't say anything to anyone. If you say anything or make a fuss . . .'

It was Nazim. He was helping her into his room. She was half-conscious with shock and anger. He sat her down gently on a chair and then sat on another, staring at the floor like a criminal. After a few moments, she was capable of thinking and understanding again. She gazed at him with loathing, then covered her face with her hands and began to sob.

'You . . . you . . . why did you bring me here from the camp?'

'I feel horrible for not being able to protect you. When Khala Bi drew a veil over one of his crimes, she gave him permission to commit another. And now he's passed the exam competition. He's starting to take control of the household. But he won't be able to bother you any more. Don't cry, Sajidah Bibi,' he said, his tone suffused with self-reproach.

'I want to protect myself. In the morning, I'll tell everyone about the enormous evil that's being nurtured here, then I'll spit on this household and leave. I don't need your sympathy. I don't need your protection. I hate you. Understand? I hate you. You forced an error in the accounts of my father's life.'

'No, Sajidah Bibi, that wasn't me! The bad accounting comes from those who are looting Pakistan instead of building it. I was just giving your Abba hints for what answers to give. And no matter how much you hate me, I'm in love with you. You're not going anywhere.'

Nazim's eyes shone with tears, but he held them back.

Sajidah stared at him in alarm and then looked down.

'You're taking advantage of the moment,' she said, bursting out sobbing.

'No, Sajidah Bibi! I want to make you my life partner. I'll turn your hatred into love and . . .' Nazim couldn't finish what he was saying because Sajidah rose from her chair and rushed to the door. She hesitated, then returned.

'Do you want me not to sit here? I can't go to my room today—everything in there fills me with fear.'

She couldn't hide her emotions. At that moment, she felt terribly alone and helpless.

'You can sleep here comfortably. Just lock the door from the inside,' said Nazim. He got up and hurried out of the room.

She spent the night sitting on the chair, weighted down with terror. That rainy night passed like the Day of Judgment. She felt as though she'd endured a torment finer than a strand of hair and sharper than the blade of a sword. If she moved at all from one side to the other, she would fall. For a moment, she wondered how there were so many versions of the bridge over hell, the *Pul-e-Siraat*, in the world, and how long she'd be able to keep her balance, how long . . .

When the damp morning light fell upon the windowpanes, she finally felt she could get up. Now she could think, and at that moment, she wondered where he had wandered, the one who had vowed to find her.

An entire night of wakefulness and mental torture had ravaged her body and soul. She came out of the room, walking unsteadily. She could hear the clang of pots and pans in the kitchen. Perhaps everyone was still sleeping because all the doors were shut. Only the dining room door was open. She peered in. Nazim was sleeping there, his head propped up on the chair. She suddenly felt sorry for him; it was because of her that he'd spent the night in discomfort.

She wanted to return to her room but shuddered at the thought that Kazim might still be there. She stood silently, leaning against Saleema's door. Now she could hear the sounds of coughing and throat-clearing coming from the other rooms.

Saleema was alarmed when she found her standing outside her door and took her into her room.

'Why were you standing out there, Sajjo? What's going on with you? Tell me.'

Saleema sat her on the bed and Sajidah lay down with legs outstretched. Her vision was suddenly blurred, and it was in this state that she told Saleema the previous night's terrifying tale. When she opened her eyes and looked at Saleema, great beads of sweat had formed on her face and her eyes were downcast. She couldn't bring herself to look at Sajidah.

'Baji, if you lower your eyes before me then whom can I look to?' asked Sajidah, sitting up and clasping Saleema's hand. 'And Baji, Nazim wants to marry me.'

'Oh!' exclaimed Saleema, as though forgetting all else. 'Really, Sajidah? I know what a good person he is. He's my brother. I've known for a long time that he's in love with you.'

'Breakfast is ready, everyone come to the table.'

Taji's voice echoed down the hallway that morning, as it did every day.

'Say yes, Sajidah! I . . . I . . .' who knows what Saleema wanted to tell her but couldn't.

Sajidah stared at her helplessly. The look of entreaty in Saleema's eyes alarmed her.

Everyone but Amma Bi was present for breakfast. Today, Kazim sat between Khala Bi and Malik. All three looked extremely pleased, as though the night's rain had made their faces bright and shiny. Taji was quickly carrying in piping hot parathas and omelettes.

'Why are you three so silent today? Do you know my son is about to get a job? The government letter has come, and he'll be made an important officer. I could barely sleep last night from happiness,' exclaimed Khala Bi, tears of joy in her eyes.

'When have you ever seen me laugh, Ammi?' Saleema retorted hotly. 'Laughter is the birthright of every human but that has been taken from me.' She stared fixedly at Kazim.

'Really, how can my brother and Saleema feel joyful right now, Khala Bi? Today, they'll be reminded of all the world's ills.'

Nazim gazed at Kazim with loathing.

'Yes, that's right, but what makes you happy gives me cause for mourning. I'm well acquainted with your future.'

'My dear brother, is it my fault if you can't make anything of yourself?' he asked, chuckling loudly.

Nazim acted as though he hadn't heard his laughter and proceeded to eat his breakfast calmly.

Sajidah glanced at Kazim and then panicked and looked down again. He was staring directly at her. The fires of vengeance smouldered in his eyes.

Malik was perhaps not completely conscious yet, or else his faculty for thought and understanding had not yet awakened. The liquor he had drunk the night before still glistened in his eyes. He spontaneously turned his head this way and that, looking around at everyone.

'Today's a day for sweets,' announced Taji, placing the tea kettle on the table. 'If you all say so, I'll heat up the pot and fry *gulguley*. Kazim Miyan is going to become an officer—oh my, I will die of happiness!' As she spoke, she stared tauntingly at Saleema and Sajidah.

'Oh, great! Taji, heat up the pot. Sajidah will also fry gulguley with you,' guffawed Kazim.

'Stop talking rubbish,' Saleema growled. 'Taji, leave the room. We don't need anything right now.'

'Oh, my, Saleema Baji. Someone merely suggested frying some gulguley and you're the one who got hit with the boiling oil!'

This was the first time Taji had ever talked back.

'What impudence!' scolded Khala Bi, turning red with anger. 'Get out of here, bitch, you're getting uppity!'

'Enough, enough, Khala Bi! Spit out your anger. Please do turn her out, but with a bit of class. I'll find her a babu-type to look after her,' laughed Kazim, glancing over at Taji.

'What greater babu is there than you now!' laughed Nazim.

Kazim acted as though he'd heard nothing, but Khala Bi started and looked at Nazim. When Taji left the room crying, Khala Bi clasped her head in her hands. 'My God! What is all this? This household wasn't always like this,' she lamented. 'You've all been strong-willed since you were small; no one listens to me. I've given everything to this household. I've sacrificed my own happiness for everyone else, but no one thinks of me.' She began to weep. 'Now I'm tired. Now I'm ready to die.' She hid her face in her hands.

'You . . . you're crying?' Malik put down his food.

Sajidah watched with alarm as tears rolled from his eyes. He got up quickly and retired to his room.

For a moment, all was still. Saleema stared at her weeping mother with a strange look. Hate, love, helplessness, madness, disloyalty: what were those emotions reflected in her eyes? Sajidah watched her with bewilderment.

'Khala Bi is returning to childhood,' quipped Kazim, opening his treasury of humour. He chuckled loudly at his own joke.

'You bastard!' Saleema screamed.

Kazim suddenly turned serious.

'Everyone is happily sitting and watching Khala Bi to see how much she can cry and I'm the one being called a bastard. This is not your mother, Saleema. She's actually my mother.' He glared at Saleema tauntingly and strolled calmly out of the room.

Sajidah got up and put her arms around Khala Bi, hugging her tightly, overwhelmed by emotion. Then she began to weep as well.

By the time Khala Bi had started patting her to calm her down, she saw that everyone else had left the room.

18

The house had been abuzz with activity since the morning. Kazim had completed his education, and his appointment letter had arrived from Lahore. He would be assigned to the rank of Sub-Divisional Magistrate forty miles away and was to assume his duties today. Malik and Khala Bi were bursting with pride.

Nazim stared hard at Kazim as he ate. Kazim looked smug.

'Oh, I forgot to congratulate you. Congratulations, Kazim!' said Nazim, as though he were self-consciously trying to prove himself the elder.

'You're congratulating me for leaving, or . . .'

'. . . for both things,' interrupted Saleema with a laugh.

'Forty miles isn't that far away. I can easily return to spend the night with everyone at home,' said Kazim as though he were announcing an important piece of news.

Sajidah glanced at Saleema nervously. Today, for the first time in two days, she'd finally sighed with relief. She'd felt a sense of freedom at the thought that Kazim was leaving. She'd become Saleema's shadow ever since Kazim had tormented her.

'Have you told my sister that you begin your position today?' asked Khala Bi fondly.

'That was the very first thing I did this morning. Amma Bi also gave me a blessing,' said Kazim.

'What was it?' asked Malik, with a laugh.

'May Allah bless you with the strength never to bring sorrow to another,' Kazim laughed.

'She's right,' said Taji, stacking hot rotis on the plate. 'The heart where God resides should never be hurt. You people don't know Punjabi. In Punjabi, if . . .'

Kazim, Malik and Khala Bi all looked at Taji and began to laugh. She became nervous and left, and Sajidah wondered if there were hearts where God did not reside and how God's residence gets destroyed time and again, and is brought to sorrow. How can human beings face God with their hearts thus wounded?

19

Sajidah had been spending her nights in Saleema's room after the incident with Kazim. If he was at home, she stayed with her out of fear. Just then, she sat alone in Saleema's room wondering what to do. Where would she go if she left? She recalled Nazim's eloquent words: 'Mr Officer rules the roost here now. Who will heed your complaints?' She could not scrub the stench of fresh blood in Taji's quarters from her mind. She wished she could scream at the top of her lungs. She hid her face in her hands with dread.

When Nazim entered the room, she calmed herself with great difficulty.

'Please have a seat,' she said in a restrained tone.

'Sajidah Bibi, what do you think? Can we not spend our lives together?' Nazim asked softly.

'Anything is possible now, Nazim Sahib,' she said hollowly. 'I just want to tell you one thing. I am in love with someone else; I don't remember for how long. I wait for him night and day.' She sighed deeply as though to save herself from drowning.

'That makes no difference to me. I'm thankful you love and do not hate,' said Nazim calmly. He didn't appear alarmed.

'I still love him. Perhaps I always will. I'm waiting for him. Please put an end to my waiting. I can no longer tolerate the agony. You do understand, don't you?' she asked, mournfully.

'How can I put an end to your waiting, Sajidah Bibi?' he asked, staring at her in confusion.

'Please put an advertisement in the papers saying, *Sajidah, daughter of the late Muhammad Ramzan, a refugee from Delhi, awaits Salahuddin, son of Alauddin. Please come and meet her at this address, wherever he may be.*'

She looked up at Nazim with lost eyes.

'I'll submit this advertisement today. God willing, he's alive and well and will quickly come to see you. Anything else?' Nazim asked.

'He must be here somewhere,' she muttered. 'He was Punjabi, but I don't remember where he lived. He had come to Delhi to study.' She started. 'Nazim Sahib, please make sure to write the correct address.' She peered at him suspiciously.

'You'll read it yourself in the paper tomorrow.'

He stood up to leave.

'I'll wait for eight days, that's it. Then, whatever you want . . .' she wept.

Nazim stopped in the hallway for a moment to wipe the tears from his eyes. He wasn't sure what emotion had inspired them.

In those days, the news was so exciting that no one was about to sit around reading advertisements. Sajidah saw the ad and folded up the paper. She hadn't even told Saleema about it. For some reason, she couldn't bring herself to mention this to her.

The ad began to run the next day and Sajidah watched the front door vigilantly. The slightest rattle startled her. 'Who is it?' she'd whisper.

Many people came and went, and her eyes stung with the anguish of waiting. She was so overwhelmed with hope and fear that she began to seem like an invalid. During that period, she stopped coming out to eat with everyone else. Saleema would force her to eat a few bites in her room and grieved at the thought that Kazim was the one who had put her in this state. Khala Bi, Amma Bi and Malik came to see her a few times. Everyone thought she was suffering from jaundice. Only Taji stared at her strangely, though she didn't dare say anything for fear of Saleema.

One afternoon, Taji brought her something to eat when Saleema was in the bathroom.

'Sajidah Baji, does your stomach ache?' Taji asked, placing her hand on Sajidah's stomach. She felt her belly, and then rubbed her hands together with disappointment.

'Do you feel better now, Taji? Can't you think of anything else?'

'Baji, when you have a stomach ache, you feel weak like this,' said Taji, brazenly ignoring her words. 'One time, I ate something unripe . . . then I got a stomach ache. My mother massaged my stomach and I was better in a couple of days, but I have no idea what you've come down with.'

'Hmph!' said Sajidah, closing her eyes.

Taji tiptoed away.

Six days had passed. Sajidah lay with her eyes closed, wondering, *Where is the one who searches for me? Where has he disappeared? Where can he be?*

Saleema stayed by Sajidah's side as much as she could. She said all sorts of things about Kazim and kept urging her to marry Nazim and she disparaged Kazim, telling her that it was she who was the honour of the family. Sajidah listened to all this and stared at her helplessly.

The eighth day of waiting finally passed; it felt like a century. And now Sajidah felt the sort of inner peace one feels on returning from a cemetery. When she got out of bed on the ninth day, her legs were wobbly. All the same, she went to eat breakfast with Saleema.

She looked up at Nazim once while drinking tea, and then looked down again. She wondered: Was she ready for this sacrifice? Were there no more miracles in this world?

Who could explain to her that reality is brutal indeed?

She set her teacup down on the table when her hands trembled, and went back to Saleema's room, ignoring everyone's questions, where she fell upon the bed as though she'd never rise again.

'Are you all right, Sajidah?' asked Saleema, following her into the room.

'I'm completely fine, Baji!' Sajidah burst out laughing. 'Please go and eat breakfast. I feel nauseous.'

'Oh! I thought maybe something was wrong.'

As soon as Saleema left, Nazim entered the room. He must have been waiting outside. Sajidah looked at him for a minute, then looked down.

'Oh, it's you,' she said and fell silent.

'Tell me your decision, Sajidah Bibi,' he said calmly, pulling up a chair and sitting down.

'You will forget everything. You will never speak Salahuddin's name, and . . .' her voice became tearful.

'All I know is that I am in love with you, and that's it. Trust me.'

'Who are you in love with?' asked Saleema, entering the room as she wiped her hands with the pallu of her sari.

They both stared back at her foolishly.

'Saleema, I want to marry Sajidah Bibi. You also hoped for this, didn't you?' Nazim asked, gazing at Saleema affectionately.

'Oh, brother! You said that so casually, as though you were saying, "I want to eat some kheer." Have you considered the storm this will unleash in the household?'

For a moment, the room was filled with silence, and Sajidah thought, *A storm will surely break out.* She was no more significant than Taji in this household. The only difference between the two was that she'd been an educated Taji when she came from the camp.

'I'm prepared for the storm, Saleema! Don't you worry. I only need to get Amma Bi's permission.' He stood up. 'I'll be right back.'

'Saleema Baji!' Sajidah cried out, trembling from head to toe.

'What is it, my darling?' asked Saleema, hugging her.

'Amma Bi . . .' Sajidah began, but she was unable to continue.

'Come with me to Amma Bi; then you'll see that she's not like everyone else,' said Saleema, grabbing hold of Sajidah's hand.

As they walked to Amma Bi's room, they encountered Khala Bi sweeping and dusting. How exhausted she looked.

She woke up at the crack of dawn and personally supervised the preparation of Kazim's breakfast, then made his lunch before bidding him farewell. Only then did she breathe a sigh of relief.

When Saleema and Sajidah entered Amma Bi's room, she was kissing Nazim on the forehead.

'Nazim, my son! This is your first and last wish, is it not?'

'Yes, Amma Bi. You can count on it.'

When Amma Bi held Sajidah's trembling head to her bosom, Sajidah fell into her arms.

'Walk quickly. Kazim may not come home tonight, so Ammi said goodbye to him and is lying sadly in her room. Taji's cooking dinner.'

Saleema held an attaché case in one hand and pulled Sajidah up from the bed with the other. Nazim stood by, watching Sajidah's face turn pale.

'For God's sake get up, Sajjo, my darling! If anyone sees us leaving the house, we'll be deluged with questions.'

Sajidah started and dragged herself up as though a deluge of questions had already drenched her. She held out her cold hand to Saleema, and the three of them walked to the old car that stood by the road near the gate.

☙

They arrived at an old mansion, where they were welcomed into a wing of the building by Nazim's friends. As Sajidah sat on a decorated bed, she noticed that the house was all done up for a wedding. She was surrounded by smiling, laughing women dressed in silks. The room was draped with red and yellow bunting, there was a wedding drum on the floor, and she could hear laughter from outside.

A little while later, everyone sat about the drum, and the singing began—classic wedding songs about a rich father with a large haveli. Sajidah sat with her head down, thinking, *Abba built a house with only two rooms, and a yard where a chameli plant grew.*

When the wedding songs were over, the film songs began:

> *Pitter-pat the clouds rain, the thrilling breezes blow,*
> *Beloved, come home, come home, beloved, come home!*

And Sajidah thought, *Amma used to say 'if a traveller begins a journey at night he will lose his way'.*

Then, suddenly, there was a great uproar.

Out of the way! Out of the way! The Qazi ji has arrived!

The women immediately hid their faces under dupattas; Saleema covered Sajidah with a shawl, and when she was asked before the witnesses if she accepted the nikah, she immediately said, *yes*—an uninfluenced *yes*; an unemotional *yes*. She couldn't even bring herself to cry the way other girls did.

In a short while, Saleema and her friend, Khurshid, had made her up and dressed her as a bride. Sajidah didn't even notice she wore the same gharara suit that Saleema sometimes wore to weddings. The necklace and earrings were also the same ones Saleema often wore.

When she was ready, a lovely woman adorned her forehead with an inlaid tikka, and Saleema whispered to Sajidah that this was Sabirah, the wife of Nazim's best friend.

'Is that what I should be called, Saleema Baji? Patience?' she murmured, touching the tikka. Saleema hugged her tightly.

She had no memory of what happened next, as though she had fallen into a deep sleep. It wasn't until the car had entered the gate, and evening was changing into the raiments of night, and Nazim had helped her out of the car, that her consciousness awoke completely.

The moment she entered the hallway, she lifted her eyes and stood tall. Today, she entered the house as Nazim's wife. She could hear Kazim talking and laughing loudly in Khala Bi's room. The tea things were set out on the table, and Taji was taking ladoos from a basket decorated with silver lace and arranging them on plates.

'Thank goodness you're all back! We were waiting for you. Kazim Miyan brought home two baskets of ladoos today,' Taji cried out enthusiastically. Then she started. 'Sajidah Baji! Did you go to a wedding? And you, Saleema Baji, you dressed so plainly.' She gazed at them in shock. 'You all went out this morning and you're only coming back now! Khala Bi has been in a state worrying about you.' She stared at Sajidah.

'Get us some nice hot tea quickly, Taji. We'll be right there,' said Nazim and they went to Amma Bi's room without waiting for a response.

Amma Bi hugged Sajidah and wept for joy. Sajidah wanted to lie against her bosom and weep but her eyes were dry.

'Go on now, have your tea. You've come home quite late; everyone was upset. Taji said that Malik and Saleema's mother hadn't eaten or drunk anything since morning.'

The three of them had only just emerged from the room when Khala Bi came rushing to see them and instantly burst into tears.

'Where were you girls since morning? Why didn't you tell me where you were going before you left?'

She rushed forward to hug Saleema eagerly but Saleema stepped back as though she hadn't seen her mother coming towards her.

'We went to a wedding. Come let's have tea,' said Saleema. She walked into the dining room holding Sajidah's hand and seated her by her side. Then, she immediately began to talk of random things. She didn't notice that her mother hung near her like a shadow.

'And you went to a wedding dressed like this! You dressed her in your clothing. If you'd told me, I could have given her my old gharara,' said Khala Bi, staring at Sajidah.

'Taji! Tea!' Saleema yelled.

'Have a little patience, Saleema Baji! Why are you yelling?' Kazim came into the room laughing. But when he saw Sajidah, he stopped in shock.

'Have a seat, Kazim. Your legs will tire from standing. And then I'll have to yell more to get you to sit down,' said Saleema.

Kazim sat down on his chair, embarrassed, but soon he fixed his gaze on Sajidah's face. Nazim and Saleema were calmly drinking their tea. Sajidah suddenly stood and glared back at Kazim.

'You, Kazim! You're so rude. You don't even know how to look at your own sister-in-law! You don't even have the manners to say hello.'

Sister-in-law. Khala Bi jumped from her chair as though a bomb had gone off in the room. Kazim, Taji and Khala Bi stared stonily at Sajidah.

'Yes, *sister-in-law*, Khala Bi! *Sister-in-law* . . .' Today, there was pride in her tone. 'Please teach your favourite some manners, or I shall break his face.'

Kazim stared at the table.

'Taji! Where is Malik? Call him. Where is he? What is this drama?' asked Khala Bi plaintively.

Taji ran out of the room.

'I've seen much drama in this house since childhood, Khala Bi. I've had enough. And I never even took part in drama at school or college,' said Nazim. He took the *nikah-nama* out of his pocket and spread it out on the table. Kazim glanced at it and then began silently drinking his tea.

The moment Malik entered the room, Khala Bi burst into tears.

'Could we not marry among our equals? But Nazim has . . .'

'. . . married the daughter of an honest munshi,' finished Sajidah, looking at Khala Bi with disgust.

'Is this true, Nazim?' asked Malik gravely.

'Yes, Malik! I'm in love with Sajidah, and I've married her. You do know that all's fair in love. I couldn't get your permission, but I believe that when it comes to love, the permission of another cannot interfere with one's happiness.

'May God keep you both happy,' said Malik. He left the room silently, and Sajidah began to pity him. No matter how long we live, we never cease to be held accountable for our behaviour.

'Yes, brother! As they say in Persian: "Each man's thoughts in accordance with his capacity." Please don't cry, Khala Bi! Do have some sweets. Taji, please serve the sweets to my dear brother and madam sister-in-law.'

'No thank you, I don't wish to be bribed for your worries.'

'Perhaps we can no longer live together, brother of mine,' said Kazim, his face turning red.

'Yes, I know,' Nazim replied calmly. 'Your brother, who used to live in small three-room government quarters, doesn't care for living in a place like this.'

'And I can't stand living with you either,' whispered Saleema.

Khala Bi looked at her sorrowfully and hid her face in her hands. She let out a muffled sob.

Kazim got up and left the room.

'Everyone please leave!' Sajidah screamed as she flung her arms around Khala Bi's neck and pressed her head to her bosom.

Nazim and Saleema got up and left like school children obeying the master's orders. Khala Bi stayed glued to Sajidah's breast, sobbing for a long time, and Sajidah thought to herself how painful it is when love turns to taunting and recrimination.

Khala Bi wept till she was exhausted. She leaned back in her chair with her eyes closed, deep in thought. Sajidah bent over and softly kissed her weeping eyes, then tiptoed from the room.

The darkness of night had descended. The light bulbs in the hallway were switched off and seemed to drown in gloom. Today, no one had remembered to turn on the lights. Sajidah walked along, slowly turning on all the switches. She saw that Taji crouched with her head on her knees in one corner of the hallway. The moment the lights came on she rose quickly and rushed away.

21

A week had passed since the wedding, but Kazim had yet to return home. Everyone knew why. Khala Bi wandered about like a madwoman, muttering softly, 'You have ruined everything, Nazim, my son!' She grew weak and was always in pain. Taji would massage her for hours but the pain simply wouldn't go away. If she got up to do some household chore, Sajidah would grab hold of her hand. Khala Bi wouldn't speak, but would go and lie in bed again.

'We've found a house, Khala Bi,' Sajidah told her one day, hoping the news would bring her some comfort. 'Tomorrow, we'll leave, then Kazim will come home everyday, so don't be upset.'

'How many times will I be murdered?' lamented Khala Bi.

Sajidah did not reply. She got up and went to Nazim's room, where she began looking through the many bundles of packed luggage that were scattered about the floor. It broke her heart to imagine leaving the house she'd threatened to leave so many times before.

The next morning, when the luggage had been loaded onto carts, she wondered how she would be able to part with everyone. Could she stand the agony? But when Nazim brought the tonga around, that task was quickly accomplished, as if it hadn't been anything at all. She didn't raise her eyes to look at anyone. She only felt the dampness of Amma Bi's and Khala Bi's tears. Taji sobbed and sobbed, and Saleema stayed in her bathroom. After waiting a long time for her, Sajidah went and sat down in the tonga. Malik stood nearby to say goodbye. He swayed as though his feet were not fixed to the ground. He'd started drinking early that morning. His bright red eyes bulged.

22

It was already evening by the time she finally had some free time after putting away the luggage in their two-room section of the old mansion. As she sat down on the bed, she felt overwhelmed by sorrow. She could hear the cries of children playing nearby and went to stand in the doorway and look outside. There was a low mud wall at a slight remove from the row of five houses. On the other side of the wall stood numerous mud houses, plumes of smoke snaking into the air from their roofs.

Attractive armchairs were arranged on the lawn of the adjacent mansion. On one of these was seated a large, fair-complexioned man, and on the other, a thin woman who spoke to him obsequiously. The man grimaced horribly. Sajidah panicked, shut the door and lay down on the bed. *Nazim should have come home early today*, she thought. A little while later, someone knocked on the door. She got up and opened it. A servant stood outside holding a tray.

'Who are you?' she asked.

'I've come from the house next door, Bibi ji! Our Begum Sahiba has sent food over, and she says if you need anything to please let her know. She'll come to see you tomorrow.'

'Please send her my greetings and thank her.'

Sajidah took the tray and set it inside. As she shut the door, she wondered who those people were and what they were like. She couldn't remember how to cook any more. When Nazim finally came home, he was embarrassed.

'There was a meeting; that's why I'm late. Please forgive me, Sajidah Bibi.'

'Food has come from the house next door. Who are those people?'

'They are important zamindars. Zamindars are rather elegant, aren't they?'

Sajidah laughed.

'But what else have they got besides that? Why don't you set out the food.'

Sajidah brought in the tray and set it down on the teapoy. Nazim spoke a great deal as he ate, and she listened silently. He had probably grown accustomed to this: he could keep talking without any expectation of a response from Sajidah, and she only spoke when necessary.

ॐ

It had been three months since they'd come to the new house, but no one from Malik's house had visited. Saleema hadn't even bothered to ask after her. She was quite shocked that they'd all forgotten her. How she wished she could visit them herself. But how could she? Kazim couldn't bear the sight of her. How could he tolerate her presence in his home? Nazim went to see Amma Bi and Saleema frequently, and he let her know how everyone was doing without her asking.

'Who knows what's happened to Saleema. She's not the same any more.' Then he turned serious. 'Khala Bi has got very weak. She starts crying as soon as she sees me. Amma Bi is lost in her own little world. Malik drinks all the time, and Kazim has had an orchard allotted in his name. You wouldn't recognize the house if you saw it now. There's always a gardener working on both lawns. Taji only does the extra work. A cook has been hired, and there are baskets of fruit lying all around the dining room. Taji always asks after you. She says I should bring her to see you some day; she's not as happy as she used to be. That house seems alien to me now, Sajidah, as though I'd never lived there. Our two rooms are much nicer than their paradise . . .'

And Sajidah kept wondering, *What has happened to Saleema? Why has she changed so much?*

The zamindar's wife was named Lali, and Sajidah had become close friends with her. She wasn't particularly well educated and was very impressed by Sajidah. Lali's life was rather strange. The Zamindar Sahib would periodically recall the forty acres of land that Lali's father had promised him for her dowry, but never given him. Then he would take out all his anger on Lali and beat her to a pulp. After she'd been beaten, Lali usually came to Sajidah. She'd examine the fresh blue bruises on her body and weep and curse her father.

Lali told Sajidah that her father had arranged her marriage in a hurry. Before the wedding, he'd given his future son-in-law false hopes and promised him all sorts of things in the dowry. But he didn't give him a single acre or even a car. He just wanted to be free of his last daughter. Not long after the wedding, he himself married an educated young woman and moved to the city, leaving Lali's mother in their ancestral haveli.

'You're so brave, Lali! You live in the Zamindar Sahib's house and love him, even though he beats you. He looks so cultured and nice, yet he does such vile things to you.'

'He has much praise for you, Sajidah Apa. He holds you up as an example and calls you his sister.'

'But he behaves in this manner towards his sister's friend?'

'No, it's just that he has a bad temper, and my father also wronged him. He deceived him,' she said, coming to his defence. 'I couldn't live in a house like the one you live in, Sajidah Apa! I don't even wash my own feet! You've seen, haven't you? There are so many servants at our house. One girl is employed just to bathe my feet.' She held her head high with pride. 'But I do sometimes think about how nice your Nazim is. He loves you; he respects you.'

Sajidah listened to her foolish words and laughed. She pitied Lali, and she was the only person who visited her and offered her companionship and sympathy in her solitude. She had begun to like her a great deal.

Five months had passed since their marriage, but not a day went by that old memories didn't torment her. There wasn't a night that thoughts of Salahuddin didn't weigh on her as she lay down to sleep. She tried to empty her head of such thoughts and throw herself into housework, but there was only so much to do in a two-room house, and whenever guests visited Lali from her village, she didn't come over to Sajidah's house for nine or ten days. Loneliness and idleness taxed her even more, and by evening, she'd be prostrate with fatigue as though she'd spent the whole day running around.

One day, she got fed up and told Nazim to enrol her in a BT degree programme. Nazim acquiesced without debate. After that, she left the house with him early every morning, locked the house, and went to college. When she came home, she'd do the housework, and by then it was evening. In this way, by her calculation, she'd been saved from the pain of her memories. But Lali was unhappy with the new arrangement. She pouted and complained about Sajidah going to college. She often insisted that she stop. 'Leave that college tomorrow, Apa! I'm so depressed without you; I feel as though I have no one at all.'

Sajidah laughed, and said, 'You get up at nine or ten, have your feet bathed until eleven, then set the servants their tasks until one. You only have spare time after that. And in the meantime, I'll be back from the college.'

'For some reason, I just don't want you to go to college and I don't like to see a lock hanging on your door,' Lali would say, and then fall silent.

23

One day she returned home from college to find fifteen or twenty men standing outside her house. They were all dressed in white. They stood about and stared in an identical fashion, just like the style of their sandals. They cleared a path for Sajidah when they saw her. When she reached the door, one of them addressed her politely: 'Begum Sahiba, do you know where Nazim Sahib might be right now?'

There was no apparent correlation between his soft tone and the harsh expression on his face.

'I don't know, perhaps he's at college.'

She unlocked the door.

'He's not at college,' another man said.

'Then I don't know where he could be. He comes home at around five or six in the evening; why don't you come and see him then?'

'All right, we'll wait right here.'

'If you wish, you may go into the sitting room.'

'Thank you, we'll stay out here.'

They moved away from the door, and she went inside, wondering what business these men had with Nazim. She'd only just changed her clothes and was walking into the kitchen when suddenly the door opened, and Zamindar Sahib came rushing in. Sajidah was shocked to see him enter like this; he only entered their house accompanied by Nazim or Lali. All the same, she politely asked him to have a seat.

'Sister! These people are police. Their cars are parked down the street; some of them are dependent on me so they didn't have the nerve to speak to you.'

'But what do they want?'

'They've come to arrest Nazim Sahib, under the Defence of Pakistan rules. I was worried about you, so I didn't go out anywhere.'

For a moment, she gazed proudly at the Zamindar Sahib, and then she looked down.

'If he's going to jail for the future of Pakistan, there's nothing wrong with that.'

'I told them to take a few thousand rupees and beat it,' he said, not really listening to her. 'But the order comes from high up; if they don't arrest Nazim Sahib, they'll be fired. I'm not sure what's to be done now.'

The Zamindar Sahib was upset, and she was astonished to find that a man who pummelled his wife over a few acres of land, beat his servants with slippers over the smallest error, and called her his sister was willing to pay a few thousand rupees for her welfare. She was pondering this when Nazim arrived. He was laughing.

'You must be upset, Sajidah Bibi. Put a few pairs of clothes in my attaché case.'

'No, I'm not upset,' Sajidah replied resolutely, and she quickly began packing his case. Zamindar Sahib was shocked to see them both so calm. Heads craned from the doors of the mansions and over the mud wall in the yard as Nazim left.

Zamindar Sahib turned towards the yard and growled, '*Oye*, you sons of bitches! Nazim Sahib isn't being arrested for theft, he's a political prisoner. You hear me? A political prisoner!'

The heads ducked behind the walls.

Sajidah gazed from the doorway until Nazim disappeared from view.

'The policemen said Nazim was being taken to Shahi Qila for interrogation,' Zamindar Sahib whispered to Sajidah.

'Shahi Qila!' She was shocked.

'Yes, sister. Many important leaders have been locked up there. They say there's better "hospitality" there nowadays than in the time of the British!'

As he was leaving, Zamindar Sahib paused for a moment. 'Sister, the ayah will come and stay here at night. Don't be frightened.'

She locked the door. A fog of stillness filled the house. She understood what was meant by 'hospitality'. She was agonized and nauseous and went to the bathroom. She felt a bit calmer after vomiting, and lay down on the bed. She realized at that moment that she hadn't told Nazim anything. How careless of her. And now she couldn't give him even that small happiness. There was no knowing how long it would be before she saw him again.

Lali came in the evening. She was worried and kept repeating. 'What crazy things has Nazim Bhai got involved in? A man should eat, drink and live comfortably. What's the point in getting mixed up in all this nonsense?'

Sajidah listened quietly as Lali comforted her as though she were a two-year-old child and then left.

The next morning, news of the arrests was printed in the newspaper. Nazim's wasn't the only name that appeared. Many others had been arrested as well; some she'd heard of from Nazim.

She hurried through breakfast and went to college as usual. When she returned, Khala Bi sat on the lone chair on the veranda, waiting for her. Khala Bi rushed to hug her when she saw her, and burst out sobbing. Sajidah reassured her a thousand times, but Khala Bi was in anguish, like a fish on wet sand. She had only one demand: 'Put a lock on the door and come with me.' Sajidah didn't want to go with her. How could she return to the house that Kazim had left because of her?

'I don't want Kazim to be forced to leave the house again,' she reasoned with Khala Bi.

'Do you think he's so evil? He was upset when he read the news. He'll do anything he can to free his brother. I was the one who brought him up. How can he be evil?'

Lali and Zamindar Sahib came to see her off. They assured her that their chowkidar would guard the house. Sajidah felt hot tears falling on her shoulder as Lali hugged her.

'Now I won't have anywhere to go when the brute beats me,' she whispered.

24

A cloud of grief hung over the house. Everyone was waiting for her. There was pride in Amma Bi's eyes when she hugged her, despite her sorrow. She told her that Nazim had spent six months in jail before the creation of Pakistan as well. Another time, Congress Party members had arrested him, but he was released after a week.

Malik called her into his room. He didn't have the strength to get up, as he'd been drinking since morning. He wept like a baby when he saw her, and kept saying: 'If only Nazim were like Kazim. He's given me such grief.'

Malik's condition saddened her. He'd drunk so much his speech slurred. His face looked distorted, like a camel's snout. She wished she could shake him. Such debased escapism clings to a man's personality like a leech. The foul stench that pervaded the room made her nauseous. When Khala Bi saw Malik's state, she tried to reason with him.

'For God's sake, have mercy on yourself! Alcohol is destroying your health.'

'What are you saying to him? He doesn't understand anything right now.'

'Dear Sajidah, I'm a poor sinner consumed by flame, but I haven't yet turned to coal or ash,' cried Khala Bi as she wiped away Malik's tears.

'If only Nazim were like Kazim, he's given me such grief,' lamented Malik.

Sajidah felt claustrophobic and left the room. She went into Saleema's room, but it was empty. She went looking for Taji and ran into her on her way to the kitchen. Taji threw her arms around her.

'Nazim Miyan used to tell me, "I'll take you to my home, Taji!" and now he's gone to jail. No one will take me away from here, Baji! No one will take me . . . but you will, won't you? You must feel so alone.'

'I've come to stay here myself now, Taji. But tell me, where's Saleema?'

'Saleema Baji,' she whispered. 'She hardly ever comes home now that you two are gone. She spends all her time with her girlfriends. She has a job, and she says she'll live at the college from now on.'

'In the hostel?'

'Yes, there.'

The house wasn't simply covered with a new patina of wealth; everything had actually changed.

She went into Saleema's room and lay down, but she couldn't shake the stench of liquor. She still felt nauseous, so nauseous it made her retch. Khala Bi's sensitive ears heard her, and she immediately came running.

'You're nauseous!' she cried. There was a gleam of joy in her eyes. 'And you also feel dizzy?'

'Yes,' she replied, looking down.

'Oh, my, Taji! Where is she?' Khala Bi went into the hallway and called out to Taji, 'Get half a lemon sprinkled with salt and bring it here.'

Then she returned.

'I hate sour things, Khala Bi,' protested Sajidah.

'Don't be shy, dear. Here, I'll get out of the way, may God release my Nazim as soon as possible,' she said, suddenly depressed. She returned to the hallway and called out, 'Taji! Hurry!'

Sajidah lay on the bed thinking. What could she say to Khala Bi who had lived through so many ups and downs herself. She'd wept copiously over Sajidah's wedding and now she was bursting with pride at the thought of her becoming a mother. How fickle is life: one's likes and dislikes get ground under foot, and it takes courage to accept all challenges with fortitude.

Taji brought her the lemon. She looked at her sadly and laughed.

'Here you go, Sajidah Baji.'

She tried to hand her the lemon wedges but Sajidah shivered.

'No, Taji!'

'Just lick it a little, Sajidah Baji. What is there to be ashamed of?' She was blushing. 'If I'm not embarrassed, then . . .'

'Taji!' she looked at her in shock.

'When Allah Miyan created poor people, Baji, he snatched all shame and shyness from them. Amma used to say, "If a poor man feels shy, how will he fill his belly?"' Taji began absentmindedly licking the lemon herself.

Sajidah's heart pounded as she remembered how Taji's quarters had reeked of fresh blood. *Oh dear, she will surely die this time,* she thought, *what a horrible state she was in that day.*

'Look, Taji, when Nazim comes back, then you come live with me.'

'Who would let me go, Baji?' she moaned. 'And anyway, Baji, it doesn't matter where the poor live, because our world never changes.'

'Taji, people aren't born poor, they're made that way. One day the world of the poor will change. Things can only get so bad. What's wrong? Kazim again?' she asked as she comforted her.

'Please don't say such things, Baji. You'll just end up getting me killed!' Taji's face turned white with fear. 'Please, don't ever say such a thing again, Baji.'

She hid her tears and ran from the room as though someone were chasing her.

'Oh, it's you, Sajjo!' called out Saleema as she shuffled in. She stood at the head of the bed and Sajidah sat up and hugged her.

'Oh, Saleema Baji! Well, I guess I know how much you love me now. I thought you could never find peace without me, but . . . ever since Nazim's arrest, I've been waiting to see only you.'

'Nazim Bhai!' Saleema sat down beside her. 'Nazim Bhai's arrest isn't at all surprising. I've been expecting the news for a long time, Sajjo. This morning, I was thinking about how the government will never let him dream of revolution. I hope they don't . . .' She fell silent. 'Taji!' she called out loudly. 'Two cups of tea.'

'I won't have any.'

Sajidah stared at Saleema in shock. How she had changed in just five months. Her always bashful face was now expressionless, as though she'd seen it all.

'Nazim Bhai must have told you that I have a job now. Time passes nicely when you're busy. I also take a music class and play badminton daily. When I come home I have absolutely no awareness of the world. I used to believe I had no talent for singing, but I actually have quite a good voice, darling,' she laughed loudly.

'I didn't come here to hear such tales from you,' snapped Sajidah. 'I just wanted to ask you this: what have you done with the love you always claimed to feel for me? All this time you never once visited me or asked how I was doing. You could have at least shown some sympathy.'

'Love, sympathy, sorrow and grief,' said Saleema, turning serious. 'All these words are meaningless to me, Sajidah Bibi! Talk about something else.'

'I know what it is, Saleema Baji. You've decided you love the company of landowners.'

Saleema must have disagreed with these words as well. When Taji brought the tea, she sat cross-legged on the bed and began sipping from her cup happily. Sajidah felt she couldn't sit there for long. She didn't want to feel bitter towards Saleema, so she went to Amma Bi's room. Amma Bi was reciting her namaz, but she entered silently and sat down on her bed. She thought about how Saleema hadn't bothered to stop her from leaving the room. What happens to humans who refuse love? They say the face of man is one of the most beautiful things in the world; how do such false sayings gain currency? The most beautiful thing in the world is the feeling of love; yardsticks for beauty are available everywhere, but there's only one for love, and it's universal. Even if people lust and steal and kill in the name of love, they cannot destroy it.

After her namaz, Amma Bi began chattering with Sajidah about this and that. Kazim returned home before Maghrib. When he saw Sajidah he immediately said hello.

'You look well, Kazim. You're getting fat; if I saw you somewhere else, I wouldn't even recognize you!'

'Really?' he laughed. 'Have you put in a request to see Nazim Bhai?'

'Yes.'

'He didn't do the right thing, but nonetheless, I assured the government that there's absolutely no connection between my views and my brother's. You can live here comfortably. You needn't worry about a thing.'

Sajidah didn't respond. Kazim stayed a few moments and then went to his room.

25

After walking all the way to the entrance, Sajidah stared up at the high trees and thick walls of the fort. She sat down on the steps, out of breath and nauseous. She'd arrived early.

'Are you all right, Bibi ji?' asked the chowkidar. 'You look pale. Don't be upset, Allah is most merciful.'

She only smiled in reply. She was thinking about how these manifestations of the architectural whims of kings had now turned into curiosities: tourists came from far off to see them; they praised their artistry and construction and attempted to read the tracery of civilizations of yore in their stones. But perhaps when they gazed upon the majesty of that edifice, they too, like her, thought about how prisoners had dwelt here before as well. Faces decorated with glittering bell-shaped tikkas and forehead ornaments, chests laden with garlands, delicate arms adorned with armlets—the obedience of slaves, the advice of advisors, bodies, hearts and minds, the emotions of love and hate—all were imprisoned here. Inside the ramparts of the fortress, festive gatherings were held with dancing and singing, at the same time as disobedient prisoners were branded in the torturer's cells. And now, centuries later, all this still took place here: festivals, encomiums . . . and torture chambers—*Attention! Make way for the king! Show respect!*—the words echoed in her ears, but now a soldier was talking to her.

'Time for the visit,' he said.

A woman walked down the stairs ahead of her, leading a small child by the hand. There were tears in her eyes and her face was flushed.

Sajidah followed the soldier into a musty old room, where a police officer was seated on a chair.

'Please come in,' he said, gesturing to another chair. He then ordered the soldier to bring Nazim Sahib in.

Sajidah's eyes were fixed on the door. Nazim entered the room a few minutes later. He walked slowly, as though he felt intense pain in his legs. He smiled when he saw Sajidah and sat down on the chair next to her.

'How is everyone?' he asked, gazing at her with love. He was smiling, but Sajidah could make out the raised bruises on his face and her heart ached.

'Everyone's well. They all miss you. I've gone home to stay with them, so don't worry about me at all. I'm busy preparing for the BT exam.'

'That's wonderful, but you look a little . . .'

Sajidah suddenly remembered that she also had to tell him the news, so he would have something to boost his courage while he was there; something to give him the will to live. She leaned over to whisper in his ear.

'Whispering is not permitted,' said the police officer.

'Very well. I just have this to say: I will soon be a mother.'

Sajidah cast a dignified glance at the police officer.

'Oh . . . Sajidah . . .' Nazim tried to rise from his chair in happiness, but the gesture made him moan with pain. 'Oh, you have to think before expressing happiness in here. Well, do look after your health. I have permission to write a letter in two weeks, and I'll write to you then,' he said affectionately.

Invisible rivers of tears seemed to flow from Nazim's eyes. Sajidah sat quietly with her head down as though there was nothing left to say. Nazim was also silent. All their unspoken words were expressed in the trembling of their lips.

'Time's up,' announced the police officer.

She stood up.

'Goodbye!' she said, gazing at Nazim's pale face. Then she turned to go.

'Goodbye! Look after yourself and say hello to everyone.'

As she was leaving with the chowkidar, she wished she could cry her heart out over the tortures being meted out to her husband—those she'd seen herself and those she'd sensed. But she couldn't shed a single tear. Her heart had been tested so thoroughly that she was now unable to weep.

26

It was like a bomb had exploded in the country. Liaqat Ali Khan had been shot while giving a speech.

'Where are these bullets coming from?' cried Malik, who was completely sober that day. Khala Bi's tears had stopped him from drinking as much.

'Don't ask me, Malik. I can't think any more. I have only one fear on my mind: What's being done to Nazim and the other political prisoners in the fortress? Only Kazim will be able to tell you what's going on. My world is in this household and that's it.'

When Kazim came home that night, Malik stood up the moment he saw him.

'What has happened, son?'

'It's simply the mischief of foreign countries,' said Kazim smugly.

'You seem to be thinking loftier thoughts this time,' whispered Sajidah.

Perhaps Kazim hadn't heard what she said. He was terribly hungry.

'Khala Bi, please serve dinner. I haven't had my lunch,' he called out.

'Why has our Pakistan attracted the evil eye?' asked Khala Bi, getting up.

'With people like Kazim . . .' Sajidah spoke softly, venting her anger. She got up and went to her room, that same room she didn't have to lock at night any more.

Khala Bi called after her, 'Sajidah, do eat something.'

'I'm not hungry, Khala Bi.'

She lay down on her bed. Saleema was out at a party somewhere and hadn't come home yet. Saleema's behaviour upset her all the time. Whenever Sajidah came home after seeing Nazim, Saleema would ask after him in passing. Sajidah would simply reply that he was fine and had asked after her. Saleema's behaviour and her indifference towards the household gnawed at Khala Bi who always pleaded with her. Instead of responding, Saleema would suddenly recall some trivial task she simply must get done. She'd dust her sheets and rearrange her chairs, or sometimes respond with, 'Mm hmm, mm hmm.'

As she lay there, Sajidah suddenly realized she hadn't seen Taji for a couple of days. Taji usually came to see her as evening fell, and stayed with her for part of the night, but now poor Khala Bi had taken on Taji's tasks, huffing and puffing in the mornings and helping out the maid. Sajidah got up and walked over to her quarters. Taji lay on her bed, battling the mosquitoes. The wick of the lantern hanging from the hook at the head of her bed was low and the room was dim. Taji's face looked dark.

'Taji,' she called out softly, 'how are you?'

She raised the wick without waiting for a response and saw that Taji's usually bright eyes were dull.

'Why are you here, Sajidah Baji? There isn't even a chair to sit on.'

'I'll sit somewhere, don't worry about me. How long have you been ill?'

'Baji, what time is it?'

'It must be around eight, Taji.'

'Eight . . .' she sighed. 'Please go now, Baji! The chowkidar has gone to call someone. Did Khala Bi not instruct everyone to go to sleep? She has a headache.'

'Who's coming? Whom did the chowkidar go to fetch?' Sajidah asked, though she sort of understood.

'I start shaking as soon as I see her, Baji. One day . . .'

'Don't worry, I'll just go and talk to Khala Bi.'

Sajidah placed her hand on Taji's hot forehead.

Taji sat up muttering in alarm, 'Don't say anything to Khala Bi; they'll kill me.' Her voice grew faint. 'It's my fault, Baji! At first, when Kazim told me he loved me, I just melted. What is this thing called "love," Baji? Khala Bi cursed me. She said I was inciting her innocent boy, but . . . now her innocent boy, her beloved officer, he swallows me whole, just like his bribes, whenever he wants, and Khala Bi . . .'

When they heard the sound of the gate opening, Taji began to shake like a leaf.

'You go, Baji! Go quickly, I beg of you. For God's sake, go,' she wept.

Sajidah could say nothing to Taji. She ran into Khala Bi when she entered the hallway.

'Where were you?' she asked, looking sharply at Sajidah.

'I went to see Taji,' she replied sternly.

'If you go into the quarters at night you might slip and fall,' Khala Bi whispered. 'May Allah keep everyone well and bring them great joy.'

Sajidah fell upon her bed. She felt anguished and worried about how Taji was being treated by that executioner of a woman whom she feared so terribly. What must Taji be going through right now! And how peacefully Kazim must be sleeping, protected by Khala Bi's love. Nobody could ruin anything for him. Perhaps it's always been thus; perhaps the weak have always been the playthings of the powerful.

She wished she could go and shake Kazim and tell him that his child was being strangled in the servant's quarters, and then she began to feel angry about this foolish notion of hers. Who calls them children? Such innocent souls are never given permission to enter the world. And if they do, humiliation follows them like a shadow.

Her anxiety exhausted her so that a sad, restless sleep rendered her oblivious for a short while. At dawn, when the faint voice of the muezzin filled the air, she opened her eyes and felt as though she hadn't slept at all. Her head pounded and she began to massage her temples.

'Are you sleeping, Sajidah?'

Khala Bi entered the room looking terrified.

'No,' she said, sitting up.

'Taji's health is very poor. What should I do, Sajidah? I'm so upset. If something happens to her . . .'

'The executioner you called, could she not do anything?'

'Please take her to the hospital,' implored Khala Bi. 'Enter the chowkidar's name as her husband.'

'No, Khala Bi! That is Kazim's job,' retorted Sajidah angrily.

'Oh, Sajidah! What are you talking about? If he took that shameless girl to the hospital—you don't know! These low-class girls are tramps. You could imprison them in a thousand walls and they still wouldn't quit. Really, what can men do around such flirts?

Sajidah wished she could beat her head, twist Khala Bi's neck, strangle Kazim.

'I won't go. Kazim will go. Kazim! Or else you will—you who play with a poor girl's life to save Kazim's honour,' she shouted.

Khala Bi clasped her hands before her.

'Don't talk so loudly. What if Malik hears? Yes, he drinks alcohol, but he has always remained pure. He will kill Kazim, or die himself, and then your Amma Bi . . . and my Kazim, whom I raised in my own arms . . .' Khala Bi burst into tears.

Sajidah longed to weep herself, but her eyes had long since gone dry. Even so, she couldn't bear to watch anyone else cry. *What if Taji dies?* she wondered. *I'd feel guilty for the rest of my life.*

'What shall I do then?'

'Do this, my darling . . .' Khala Bi wept as she spoke. 'The driver is ready, get the gardener and Taji into the car, and go to the hospital.'

She didn't respond. She hurriedly combed her hair and rushed to Taji's quarters. Khala Bi ran after her. She could hear Taji's breathing. She lay unconscious in her room, the dim yellow light of the lantern illuminating her face.

'Taji!' Sajidah called out.

Taji did not open her eyes.

'Oh, Bibi ji! Are you bringing up the hospital too?' asked the midwife nervously. 'I do thousands of cases. She'll toss and turn and be better by morning. Just let me go home. I'll give her four doses of medicine and that'll stop the bleeding.'

'And if she dies, you won't be going home, you'll be going to the police station,' said Sajidah, glaring murderously at her. 'Pick up the cot.'

The midwife stared at Sajidah and shrank back. Then she and the gardener grabbed hold of the cot and carried it out to the car.

℘

Taji's nocturnal assailant slept peacefully in his own bed as Sajidah paced back and forth outside the operation theatre, praying for the poor woman's life.

After resting in a bed in the general ward for two or three days, Taji was finally able to return home. Sajidah was reminded of the yellowing decay of autumn leaves when she saw her. Taji was silent now, and lost, as though the last few drops of blood had been wrung from her, taking with them her ability to speak, think and understand.

27

A letter had come from Nazim, in which he'd written:

> *These days, I keep re-reading the books you gave me. They're so valuable to me, even just to pass the time. If someone had told me under happier circumstances that I would get a prize for reading them, I probably wouldn't have done it. Tales of love and romance in which women are neglected in so many ways—they're not the kind of thing I usually read, but these too are classics. I hope you have received those books that did not quench my thirst for knowledge, or were not worthy of my reading. During moments of leisure, I get lost imagining our tiny boy or girl. The child will take after you, or after me. Please look after your health and take care of my treasure; I can't tell you how much I miss you. Greetings to everyone.*

She went to visit him every two weeks, and each time, he looked weaker than before. He was losing his health and had grown thin and sallow.

Back at home, she lay with her face covered for hours. Amma Bi, Khala Bi and Malik would try their best to learn more about Nazim. *How is he? What did he say? Is he fed properly?* She told everyone the same thing: *He's fine. We can't talk about much in there. He asks after everyone.*

At night, after Taji's work was done, she'd come and sit by Sajidah and speak fondly of the baby.

'Make a soft little pillow for the baby, Sajidah Baji. And a quilt and a mattress—all should be silk, and yes, do sew the baby darling little lace clothes. Oh, how cute it will look! Who knows who it will take after—you or Nazim Miyan!'

Sajidah would laugh as she listened to Taji. But one night, when Taji came into her room after finishing her housework, she held something wrapped in a clean handkerchief close to her chest.

'Here, Sajidah Baji, I sewed it with my own hands. I ordered the fabric through the gardener. It's not that nice but . . .'

Sajidah sprang upon the little package as though she were dying to see it.

She held up a tiny blue satin kameez-like creation stitched with white thread from the collar to the hem.

'Oh, Taji! What a sweet kameez it is! Did you truly stitch it yourself? I can't believe it.'

Sajidah quickly put it away in her trunk. Taji's eyes shone with tears.

'Tell me something, Baji,' she said sadly. 'Will you let me hold the baby?'

'Why, of course! Why wouldn't I?'

Taji suddenly hid her face in her hands and ran away sobbing.

Sajidah felt a shock in her very soul, as though there'd been an earthquake, as though the walls and doors of her body and soul might shudder and fall and no one would be there to help. A little while later, when she felt calmer, she called out weakly, 'Taji!'

28

Khala Bi stayed with her in the hospital for a week. Sajidah was deliriously happy when she gazed upon her tiny plump baby boy. She still felt joyful when she returned home. Malik spoke to the baby affectionately: 'I'm your Gwandfather! I'm your Dada! Do you wecognize me?'

When everyone in the house was busy, Amma Bi went into Sajidah's room and showered the baby with love. She held out her hands in prayer for Nazim's return. Saleema never came home until late at night, and locked herself up in her room when she did. But nowadays she also came to see the baby for a few minutes. When Taji came to hug the baby, Khala Bi handed her his dirty diapers and she went away quietly.

Sajidah missed Nazim terribly when she was alone. Nazim, who was her child's father, and who had written in a letter: *I keep imagining myself coming home, and how I'll give him his name with your advice. I've thought of many good names in jail, names I like very much. Sometimes it seems as though names become a mirror of one's personality.*

That afternoon, when she was alone, she stared at her baby for a long time, trying to decide whom he resembled more.

Suddenly, she felt that his forehead looked like Salahuddin's. After that, the more she looked at the baby, the more his features seemed to resemble Salahuddin's. She heard footsteps by the door as she hugged him tightly to her breast. Kazim stood hesitantly in the doorway.

'Come in, Kazim. Why are you standing there? Come in. I always look for the good side of even my bitterest memories. And just think, if you hadn't considered me a Taji, I might never have become your sister-in-law or met this tiny baby. When he touches the wounds of my heart, with his tiny hand, I . . .' She fell silent.

Kazim approached the child, head down, as though he had forgotten everything else.

'Hey mister!' he said, grabbing the baby's hand with a finger and shaking it. 'Oh, Bhabhi, he looks exactly like my brother!'

Sajidah laughed, embarrassed. What had she been thinking just a short while ago? Babies take many forms before their facial features truly emerge.

'Yes, he looks exactly like your elder brother,' she said.

'Hey, little Miyan, you're just like him, but don't be like him when you grow up. Be like me and you'll be happy. This is it, Bhabhi! I'm going to get married too. Seeing this baby makes me feel like having a son of my own.' He chuckled heartily, picking up the baby and showering it with affection.

'Maybe the other babies that were snuffed out in the dark were sons too,' snapped Sajidah.

Kazim laughed insolently.

'Fancies about morality have made Saleema Baji useless. Don't you fall into that trap too. If I hadn't made use of Taji, then someone else would have. She was born into the world for just that purpose. She eats and drinks happily, laughs and plays. What else could she want? Thoughts about relatives or ties probably don't even occur to her tiny imagination, and here you are trying to force a reckoning for the deaths of those sons. Babies like that lie rotting on heaps of trash, in rivers and in sewers. No one keeps track of their deaths at all.'

He was angry now. He put the baby down in front of Sajidah and left the room.

'Listen to what I have to say, my brother!' she called out after him, but Kazim was too far away to hear her words.

'You're evil!'

Calling Kazim evil made her feel a bit better.

29

Nazim was finally freed and returned home that day. He'd grown so weak he was unrecognizable. Saleema was at a friend's house as usual. Khala Bi, Malik and Taji gathered in Sajidah's room. Kazim arrived soon after. The two brothers greeted one another formally, their eyes devoid of family feeling. Nazim held the baby and kissed it over and over, but he could only stand for a few minutes at a time. Then his legs began to shake, and he'd panic and sit down.

'You're quite weak, dear brother! Please know that I worked covertly to get you released.'

'Thank you. You've become a Deputy Commissioner at such a young age. It was the least you could do since you live in this city. But anyway, for your information, I must tell you that my prison term had ended.'

'Do not speak of prison terms, brother. You know full well how these terms have a way of getting extended.'

'This is a time to be happy. Don't talk of foolish things,' Khala Bi chided Kazim for perhaps the first time, and he stared at Nazim as if to curse his ingratitude. But Nazim was lost in his child.

'I wrote to you, Sajidah, that when I came home, I would give the baby a name. So, listen, his name will be Asad. Here, take Asad now. My arms hurt.'

'You should have asked Malik to name him. You didn't even ask him,' scolded Khala Bi.

'No matter, no matter. When children grow up, they are masters of their own wills, and then, I—all the children, really . . .' What was Malik trying to say?

'A dear friend of mine is named Asad. I like him very much. He's brave and heroic and courageous.'

'Where is he now?' asked Kazim, eyeing Nazim slyly.

'Over there, in that cattle pen, where "dog cells" have been created for humans. Understand, Kazim Miyan?'

Kazim chuckled and looked at his watch.

'I have to get to the club,' he said and left.

Nazim stared angrily after him.

'Don't be angry, Nazim Miyan. You look so unhealthy now,' said Taji, adjusting the dupatta on her head. She burst into tears.

'Enough, enough, you act as though you carry everyone's sorrows in your heart. There's no need to make a show of sympathy. Go on, go do your work. My son will be shipshape in a few days,' chided Khala Bi.

Everyone had left the room. After a little while, Amma Bi stopped by briefly to bless her son. Sajidah suddenly panicked. Nazim dragged his emaciated body to sit beside her. His legs were in horrible pain and he favoured one leg when he walked. She pitied him, just as she always had since marrying him.

Nazim placed his cold face against hers.

'Because of you, I had no choice but to go on living in there . . .' he said, overcome with emotion.

'Forget all those things for now. We'll go back to our house tomorrow with our very own Asad,' said Sajidah, holding his face in her hands. 'I'll get a job and you can rest for a while.'

'Can you be happy there after spending so much time in this splendid mansion? The entire appearance of this house has changed. When you enter through the gate and look at the lawn it's like entering Lawrence Gardens.'

'Being here fills me with dread,' said Sajidah, and she told the entire tale—of the untimely deaths of Taji's babies, of Khala Bi's anxiety over Kazim's honour, of Saleema's detachment from the household, of Malik's drinking. And she told him that Malik believed once Nazim returned from jail, his views would change, that he'd cooperate with his brother, and thus the household would be joyful again, and no longer feel empty. Saleema would also begin to take an interest in the house, because she only listened to him.

'And Taji says she'll come with us,' she added.

Nazim listened quietly, but his expressions changed as though he were experiencing extreme agony.

'I cannot live here. I can't live in such a house for even one day, believe me, Sajidah. I didn't break the lock on this house. A house that has been broken into belongs to no one. How can I live in this home we don't own! And yes, I'll try to take Taji with us.'

'Malik is calling you, Nazim Miyan,' announced Taji, entering with her gaze downcast.

She left and Nazim slowly walked out of the room.

30

The next evening, as they all sat in chairs on the lawn, Kazim enumerated his accomplishments and Malik chuckled at everything he said. Taji brought out the tea, and just as they picked up their cups, Nazim told them that he and Sajidah would be returning to their own home the next day.

'Why?' cried Malik, nearly dropping his teacup.

'Do the comforts and beauty of this immaculate home not suit you?' asked Kazim gravely.

'Bring a naked, hungry man to a beautiful place. What do you think, how will he like it?' He paused to take a breath. 'When Taji steps onto this flower-filled lawn, don't you feel that autumn is around the corner and with it, the stench of blood . . .'

Khala Bi shrank back and glanced at Nazim. 'Bhai Miyan!' interrupted Kazim, 'Clearly, there's no autumn where you live. Me, I think only of my father, Khala Bi and Saleema.'

'I wish to take Taji with me as well . . .'

'She is our household servant. She cannot go with you.'

'For God's sake, both of you be quiet. I'll arrange for an ayah for Asad Baba,' said Khala Bi, her voice shaking. 'We had hoped to be happy for just a little while, but it's impossible. Nazim, my son,' she cried, bursting into tears.

'Why do you hate us?' asked Malik. He stood up and quietly walked away. At that moment, Sajidah felt great pity for him as a father.

'I don't hate anyone, Khala Bi!'

'You've separated from us; Saleema has become distant.' Khala Bi wiped her eyes. 'No one thinks of me . . . I . . .'

'You come with me too,' said Sajidah. She couldn't stand to see her tragic expression.

'You want me to leave this house now, at this age? I will only leave when I'm carried out on four shoulders,' she said, getting up and rushing away as though she'd just remembered something she had to do.

Sajidah watched her leave. Today, it seemed to her that Khala Bi's heavy body had shrunk to half its former size. Her pale complexion had turned sallow.

Nazim was holding Asad in his arms, gazing at him entranced, when Saleema walked in through the gate. She hesitated slightly when she saw Nazim. Then she quickly walked over. 'Thank goodness, Nazim Bhai, you've come home.'

'What do you care whether I'm coming or going?'

'Oh, come now, Nazim Bhai! Please let's speak of more important topics. Do such petty things really matter?'

As Saleema turned to leave, Sajidah searched for some emotion in her eyes, but her flat expression betrayed nothing.

The next day, Sajidah rolled up the bedding and packed the suitcase. As she was about to pick up Asad and leave, she suddenly heard scuffling from Malik's room. The alcohol was making him stammer, as he screamed, 'Go away, everyone, leave! Take my grandson from me! What are these gardens and orchards for? Who will eat these fruits? Who will play in these rooms?'

Khala Bi was taking care of him and comforting him, but the alcohol had possessed him so that he was incapable of any thought or understanding. When Nazim and Sajidah came into the room carrying Asad, Malik lay unconscious on his bed, staring at them glassy-eyed. Sajidah was alarmed. She gave Asad to Nazim and quickly left the room. Saleema stood in the hallway with her back against the wall. When she saw Sajidah she said, 'Holidays are intolerable in this house.'

'Saleema Baji, you're tormenting Khala Bi!' she blurted out. 'You should know how much a mother yearns.'

'Who's tormenting whom, really? Ah well. So, you're leaving today?'

'Yes.'

'Did you go and see Amma Bi?'

'We both sat with her for a long time; we left only after she had given us her blessings.'

'Hmmm.'

'Where's Taji? I'm leaving and she's missing. She hasn't come to see me.'

Sajidah didn't want to talk to Saleema about anything else. She turned swiftly towards Taji's quarters and missed the peculiar smile on Saleema's face as she watched her walking away.

When she found Taji, she was sitting with her face buried in her knees, softly singing:

Two pomegranate leaves,
Hear my cries of sorrow,
Even the rocks on the mountains weep . . .

Sajidah stood silently for a moment, then she called out softly, 'Taji!'

Taji stood up from her charpoy, her eyes pink from weeping.

'I know, Baji, you're leaving.'

'I'll definitely have you come to our house one day,' said Sajidah.

Taji laughed sadly. 'Yesterday evening, before going to the club, Kazim Miyan stopped by. He slapped me hard across the face and said that when he got married, he'd pick me up and drop me at Nazim Miyan's house, but right now, if if I made so much as a peep, no one would even get my corpse.' Her eyes darted about. 'Am I alive now? Anyway, I'll come to see Nazim Miyan off, and give Asad my love. You're doing the right thing by leaving. This is a cursed house, Sajidah Baji.'

Taji spoke as she walked along with Sajidah who was thinking only of Kazim. What would happen if people like Kazim continued to hold positions of power in this pure land? By now he'd become a tiger, fearing no one.

Khala Bi and Taji bid Sajidah farewell with tears in their eyes.

'Leave! Everyone leave!' Malik continued to bellow. 'Who will eat the fruit from my orchard?'

And Saleema stayed where she was, back pressed against the wall. When the tonga left, she waved and then her arm fell lifelessly to her side.

31

Lali and Zamindar Sahib were delighted at their return. In the evenings, Nazim sat and debated for hours with Zamindar Sahib on his lawn. Zamindar Sahib stuck to his belief that all people were God's creations: the great and the small, the rich and the poor; and Nazim kept trying to make him see that God had created mankind, but the boundary between small and great had been created by man, as was the case with the rich looting the poor. The labourers on his lands provided him with such luxury, but look at their conditions: they long for even a little happiness.

One day their conversation took a bitter turn, with Zamindar Sahib arguing loudly, 'You speak of the rights of the poor, but if they get hit over the head a couple of times with a staff, they will completely forget all this "rights" nonsense.'

'And Zamindar Sahib! If the staff were to turn around, and . . .' Nazim replied angrily. 'But blind thinking does not allow for foresight.'

'If you continue to hold such views in Pakistan, you'll spend your whole life in prison.'

After this bitter argument, Nazim did not visit the Zamindar Sahib any more, and Lali did not come over.

Nazim was still so weak that he lay in bed all day long, distracting himself by reading books and newspapers and playing with Asad. His stomach and liver had both weakened in jail. In the meantime, Sajidah had got a job in a nearby school and they managed to get by on her salary. Sajidah was feeling ill once again, but she said nothing to Nazim. She didn't want to upset or burden him. She felt her heart break when she saw him limping.

What with housework, looking after the baby, teaching, and caring for Nazim, she had no time for forgotten memories. The anti-Qadiyani movement was intensifying, so the schools and colleges had been closed. This gave Sajidah the opportunity to spend most of the day at home. She didn't let on to Nazim that she felt afraid. One day, she was heating up the food when someone knocked on their door. Her heart began to pound. What if Nazim had received another summons! Her heart pounded horribly with every knock.

When she opened the door, Zamindar Sahib stood before her. He patted her affectionately on the head.

'You may get angry, but I must take care of my sister. Where is Nazim?'

'Please come in, Bhai Sahib,' she responded joyfully and took him to Nazim, who was reading the paper and looking worried.

'There's been terrible rioting against the Qadiyanis. Have you read the news? Many people have died, shops have been looted, and look at the police—they're shooting at their own people. I mean, let them loot the Qadiyanis. They're not Muslims. Our government has crossed the limit. It has arrested many pious scholars while protecting these cursed people,' blurted out Zamindar Sahib.

'It is true that these pious scholars should finish off all the world's *kaffir*s, but Zamindar Sahib, hell must be quite large if all these people are going there. Paradise is only for Muslims like you, right?'

'Please, Nazim Sahib! This is no time for jokes.'

Suddenly, they heard loud cries from the yard. Sajidah panicked and went to the door. A blood-soaked body was being carried into the yard, where it was laid out on a charpoy, and women had gathered around, wailing in mourning. They pounded their breasts and cried to the young men: 'Go! Take revenge! Kill ten martyrs for each body!'

Sajidah began to feel dizzy. The blood, the riots, Delhi's galis, the refugee camps—it all flashed before her eyes. She managed to steady herself and return to the room.

'What happened?' asked Nazim, helping her into a chair.

'A corpse was brought in, drenched in blood . . .' she leaned back in her chair, closing her eyes.

Nazim quickly switched on the radio. Martial law had been declared in Lahore. The martial law regulations were being announced on the radio. Nazim closed his eyes.

'The horrifying actions of incompetent rulers.'

Zamindar Sahib stood up to leave.

'I'm going home to see what's happening. My servants came out to see what was going on. Damn them! I don't want them killed for nothing.'

'Don't you worry, bullets recognize even the servants of zamindars,' joked Nazim. But Zamindar Sahib left without a reply.

The cries of mourning frightened her. Sajidah thought
about how difficult it was for the poor to raise their children,
and how quickly they were pushed towards death. And those
doing the pushing didn't get so much as a scrape. The crying
continued all night long. She had given Nazim his sleeping
medicine to help him rest, but she herself tossed and turned
all night, plagued by disturbing thoughts that invaded her
mind like evil spirits. Once or twice she even wondered: *What
must our Deputy Commissioner be doing these days? How pleased
he must be by this festival of blood!*

In the morning, only nine or ten men were willing to
lend a shoulder to carry out the bier for fear of martial law.
The shrieks and cries of the women had also subsided into
sobs.

'Let's hope this martial law doesn't turn into a dark
portent of the future,' Nazim worried.

Sajidah listened to him silently as she paced anxiously
back and forth through the two-room house.

'Why don't you rest a while,' he suggested.

This made her angry. 'If you can't do anything, what's the
point . . .'

Nazim lay down quietly on the bed with an air of defeat.

When the horror of martial law had diminished, more
important news was announced. Chief Minister Daulatana
Sahib had resigned from his post.

'How many ministers have been dismissed since Pakistan
was created. What minister has resigned this time?' Nazim
asked vacantly.

'I don't remember,' Sajidah replied apathetically, as she
changed Asad's clothes.

That evening, Nazim's friends came over. Suddenly, the room was full of voices. There was a heated discussion about martial law and Daulatana's resignation. Sajidah quickly prepared tea and laid it out on the teapoy so that she could listen to what everyone was saying in peace. They all spoke at once—it was their first opportunity to speak on the subject—but Nazim sat quietly.

'Does martial law still bother you?'

'Nothing bothers me at all,' Nazim replied softly. 'I'm listening to what all of you have to say. But let me tell you this: Daulatana did not resign. Defence Secretary Sikandar Mirza made him write out his resignation so that it would look as though he came from Karachi on a bet with someone. Then, he waved the piece of paper from the balcony of Government House, and poor Khwaja Nazimuddin only later learned that martial law had been announced. He's only prime minister in name.'

Silence fell in the room. Perhaps everyone was thinking about how the rule of bureaucracy would wreak havoc now. Just then, there was a light tap on the door and everyone started.

'You all shouldn't come to my home now,' said Nazim. 'I'm like a beaten pawn lying helplessly on the board. Don't get tangled up in disaster for nothing. If you are tortured after actually doing something, that will at least give you some peace.'

'I'll see who it is,' said Sajidah.

She went to the door.

'Who's there?' she called out.

'Lali.'

Sajidah quickly opened the door and Lali came in.

'Your brother says the CID is after Nazim Sahib now, so you shouldn't hold such large gatherings on quiet evenings with everyone speaking loudly. Voices carry. And here are some sweets. Nazim Bhai still can't walk around properly, so please serve them to your guests with tea.' She handed the box of sweets to Sajidah and left immediately.

'Who was it?' Nazim asked.

'Lali came with sweets for our guests, and she also said that voices carry on quiet evenings.'

'It can't be that your Zamindar Sahib is spying on us, can it?' Nazim asked worriedly. 'No, he wouldn't do such a thing. If I were to clash with him he would of course become my enemy. But why would he make enemies with an ordinary person like me? Maybe he does understand a bit more after debating the state of the country with me.'

Perhaps the sweets were bitter, because everyone left in a few minutes. Sajidah locked the door and lay down on the bed with Asad. Nazim seemed lost in worry.

'Can I ask you something?' said Sajidah softly.

'Ask away.'

'What did they want to know from you at the fort?'

'Everything they already knew.'

'Like what?'

'Like whether I believe in democracy, justice, and equality, and if I'm against limitations on free speech, and whether I criticize the government.'

'And what's wrong with that?'

'They don't understand that there's no chance I'll become an assembly member, or that I'll gain possession of even one acre of land through intercession, or that I'll influence agrarian reforms. So they can't figure out who's directing me to support democracy and equality and interfere in the government's work,' said Nazim, as though speaking to himself. 'They also disliked the fact that I dream of making Pakistan a model country and support its survival and progress. All these things carry a stench of conspiracy for them, and they wanted to know more about it.'

'And then?'

'And then, when I assured them that I, like them, also consider Pakistan manna from heaven, and plan to enjoy it, they ceased to torture me, and I was released.'

'Is that really true, Nazim?'

'No, but I no longer had the strength to endure more. After all, how long can a man lie on a block of ice and . . .' he stopped for a moment. 'A man can lie to get released, which is better than staying in prison. Do you have anything else to ask?'

'No.'

They were silent for a long time.

A mile or so beyond their home was a wasteland, with no sign of human habitation, where one could hear the howling of jackals at night. This woke Asad, and as Sajidah held him to her breast, she saw Nazim staring at her vacantly, with haunted eyes. Sajidah felt ashamed of her questions and closed her eyes. For a long time, she could feel Nazim tossing and turning beside her.

32

After coming home from school, looking after two little boys so close in age, and doing all the housework, Sajidah was so tired each night that she fell asleep the moment she lay down. Sometimes she'd wake up, see Nazim bent over the small second-hand table writing, then turn over and go back to sleep. She woke at the crack of dawn each morning, prepared breakfast, changed Asad's and Ahmad's clothes, then turned them both over to Nazim and went to work. Nazim had yet to find a job, and by now their link with Malik's home seemed completely broken. When Ahmed was born, only Khala Bi had come to see them. She had grown very weak. She sat for a long time weeping, as she told them that Malik had sworn never to visit Nazim's home, and that he would not allow anyone from the household to go either. Nazim had thrown away his love and separated himself from them. There wasn't any question of visiting Nazim. But yes, the door to their home would remain open to him, and he could come whenever he liked. And Nazim, despite Sajidah trying to stop him, had told Khala Bi with loathing to tell Malik that he could go ahead and lock all the doors, and just to leave his mother's door open.

'I'll go and see my mother, but no one will ever know when.'

'And you won't visit me?'

Khala Bi's voice was full of longing. Nazim did not reply. He was busy playing with Ahmed. For a few minutes, Khala Bi watched Nazim sadly and then began to talk to Sajidah. She said that Saleema now lived in the hostel; she was disgusted by her mother's love. Kazim was interested in a girl; he was taking her to the club these days. The girl's father was a rich man, and Kazim said the girl was genteel like her family. Taji missed them both a great deal and cried a lot.

Sajidah watched Khala Bi's face as she talked on and on, and felt as though all the sorrow of the age was captured in her eyes. Her ravaged face seemed to take the form of a question mark, asking what had been lost and what found. Khala Bi extracted a promise from Sajidah before she left, that she would visit the house from time to time even if only for an hour or two. It would bring her some happiness and make her feel as though Saleema had come to see her.

'Don't you ever visit Saleema?' Sajidah asked.

'I've gone several times, but every time I visit her, she says she's happy there, and tells me not to leave home or an earthquake might come and toss the whole house up in the air. But, of course, I know that, my dear,' she said, then stared into the void.

Sajidah recalled her Hindu girlfriend who used to say that a cow balanced the earth on its horns, and that whenever it changed horns there was an earthquake.

What does Saleema get out of being sarcastic to her own mother? Sajidah thought after Khala Bi had left. She thought about Saleema for a long time. Despite her heedlessness, Sajidah still loved Saleema.

33

When Lali came over that afternoon, her face was flushed and her eyelids swollen. She stumbled in and threw herself on the bed as though she didn't have the strength to stand. Then she burst out sobbing.

'What happened, Lali?' asked Sajidah, hugging her. 'Please say something.'

'The same thing that always happens. Today, he once again remembered those acres of land that my father refused to give him after we got married.'

'And then?'

'And then he cursed my father. I said to him, "Whatever my father may be, don't curse him in front of me, that's all I ask . . ."'

'Why don't you go to your family home for a while. If you're not here, the old scoundrel will be put on notice.'

'I have no family home. My mother died, my father's remarried, and my brother is master of one hundred twenty-five acres, but he fears he might be forced to give me something. Wealth is a serious matter, Baji. He has four grown sons and I don't even have any children, but he told his sons, when he was arranging their marriages, that they would each get a servant girl, and twenty to thirty acres of land as well.'

'Look, Lali,' said Sajidah, sitting up. 'You're not even educated. What I mean is, you don't even have a degree. You have no means to gain independence. Yes, you are young and beautiful. Zamindar Sahib will never leave you in old age, but he'll also never give up this property dispute. And he does love you; otherwise he wouldn't live with you separately from the rest of his family. He spends the income of five or ten acres of his land on this household and servants alone.'

'Then, what should I do, Baji? I'm tired of being beaten. All my happiness has turned to sorrow. Where can I go?' She began to cry again.

'If you cry, I won't help you,' complained Sajidah, looking away.

'Then what should I do?' Lali quickly wiped her tears.

'This is what you should do: when he hits you, you hit him right back.'

'I hit him?' Lali's eyes grew wide with astonishment.

'Yes, you. He'll keep hitting you as long as you keep putting up with it, but once you raise your hand against him . . .'

'He won't throw me out of the house?' asked Lali, frightened.

'He'll never throw you out, and if he does, I will support you for the rest of your life. I'll wash your feet. I'll comb your hair, and . . .'

Lali burst out laughing, and as soon as the servant came to get her, she left.

Sajidah was worried. What would happen if Lali actually heeded her advice? What if he really threw her out? But then she felt calmer when she thought about how Lali would never do such a thing. Wealth is a balm that heals all wounds.

She wanted to sleep for a long time, but then Nazim came home, looking happier than usual. The moment he walked in, he told her he'd got a job at a weekly magazine; the pay was low, but he would no longer be unemployed.

'You were worrying too much about your unemployment; our household wasn't suffering.'

'I've felt nothing but joy living with you, Sajidah,' he said, gazing at her with such love that she had to look down.

'But, but . . . I'm not so very nice. I'll make you some tea.'

She got up from the bed. Even after all this time, Sajidah still made a conscious effort to avoid Nazim's amorous glances. She wondered how he could still love her, even after knowing everything. He'd never mentioned Salahuddin. Like love, hate, too, can sometimes be blind. The man she hated was wonderful—all the same, she was unable to love him, despite her best efforts. She couldn't think of him as anything more than the father of her children.

Her heart overflowed as she made tea. She wished she could cry. But her eyes were now permanently dry.

'Today, I went to see Amma Bi; she spoke fondly of you,' Nazim told her as he drank his tea.

'Did you not see Khala Bi? I heard she was ill.'

'No, I couldn't. I didn't want Malik to know I was in the house.'

Sajidah was silently blowing on spoonfuls of tea and feeding them to Ahmed when someone knocked on the door. Nazim went outside and didn't return until she was sound asleep. Her eyes opened when she heard a repeated knock on the door, and when she opened it, Nazim stood there ashamed.

'I had to write an article. The magazine is going to press in the morning.'

'Will you eat?'

'No, you go to sleep. I've just eaten.'

34

When she came home from school that day, she found the gardener standing at the door, looking worried.

'Baji! Please come home. Khala Bi asked me to get you.'

'What's wrong?' asked Sajidah, staring at him in panic.

'Just that . . . just come home, the tonga is waiting.' The gardener wasn't prepared to answer.

Sajidah quickly unlocked the door, put the children's bags inside, and then locked it again.

'You two go play at Aunty Lali's house. I'll be back in a little while,' she said.

She led them quickly by the hands to Lali's house, where she gave Lali the key and told her to tell Nazim when he came back that she had gone to the family home, and that the gardener had come to get her; she'd return by evening.

'Please look after the children in the meantime, my sister,' she pleaded.

Lali asked her all sorts of things, but Sajidah heard nothing. She ran outside and sat down in the tonga. She was plagued with horrible thoughts the whole way. What if Khala Bi's health had taken a turn for the worse, or something had happened to Malik? Sometimes he drank so much it seemed like he'd breathed his last.

When she reached home, Khala Bi stood by the gate, clutching weakly at the wall. She embraced Sajidah.

'Come to my room,' said Khala Bi.

She dragged herself along and could only make it with Sajidah's help.

'Sajidah, I must once again ask you to save this family's honour! Taji is in terrible shape. She's dying. Please take her to the hospital.'

Sajidah didn't stop to ask questions. She went running to Taji's quarters where she found her lying semi-conscious, her face swollen.

'Taji!' Sajidah leaned over her. Taji's lips moved slowly in response, but Sajidah couldn't make out what she was saying.

The gardener was wiping away tears with the end of his turban.

'What can anyone say to rich folk, Sajidah Bibi. The poor can only see but not hear. We don't have a tongue in our heads, Sajidah Bibi! How much better it would be if Allah had made us mute from birth!'

'Mali! Now is not the time to talk about such things. Quick, grab the cot and take it to the car.'

They lifted the cot together and carried it to the car. The gardener and driver laid Taji out on the back seat, and Sajidah rested Taji's head in her lap.

'She must be pretty fancy for a two-bit girl to have the Sahib send a car for her!' said the driver.

'Stop talking nonsense, and drive quickly,' Sajidah retorted. She knew that Kazim's driver was the same man who called out the names of the indictees and petitioners outside his court, and that the two of them filled their pockets with bribes before coming home every evening.

When the car made its way through the hospital gate, a bell sounded. Two men rushed to the side of the car with a gurney. As Sajidah ran alongside the gurney, she caressed Taji's cold face and watched her lips moving. No one knew what she was saying, no one listened, no one stopped to see her.

In a short while the gurney stood in the corner of the emergency ward. They learned that the doctor was currently drinking tea after performing an operation. Sajidah paced anxiously, then stopped to lean over Taji. Her expression was unstable as though she was slowly sinking.

'Taji . . . Taji . . .!' Sajidah whispered into her ear.

Taji's eyelids fluttered open once as though the burden of centuries of toil weighed them down.

'What are you saying, Taji . . . what?'

She closed her eyes again. Her black cracked lips were still moving. Sajidah leaned forward to listen. Her breathing was shallow as she murmured, 'Amma . . . I didn't find an honest hand. Amma! I didn't find it, I didn't find anyone, I . . .' her voice sank again.

'Taji . . . Taji! What are you saying?' cried Sajidah, but now Taji's lips refused to move.

'Sister!' Sajidah screamed. She grabbed the nurse by the shoulders. 'Where is the doctor? When will he be done with his tea?'

The doctor emerged from his room and stood before Sajidah.

'This is a hospital; you're making too much noise,' he admonished with a frown. 'Are we not human? Are we not permitted a few sips of tea?'

'Doctor Sahib! You . . .' Sajidah could say nothing.

The doctor leaned over Taji and checked her pulse.

'Doctor Sahib, you don't recognize me. My name is Sajidah. My father died in the camp; you were at the camp in those days,' she said tearfully. 'Please save Taji, Doctor Sahib.'

The doctor turned to look at her with disgust. It was insulting to remind a famous gynaecologist of the camps.

'She's already gone,' he declared coldly. The nurse came forward and pulled the sheet over Taji's face. 'You people only think of the hospital after you've finished the patient off at home.'

He returned to his office.

Sajidah wept with shock as she completed all the paperwork. She stared at the gardener in a daze.

On the way home, the gardener wept, and whispered, 'Sajidah Bibi, I feel as though Taji really was my wife. I fear my heart will break. Why did you people always give them my name? Why?' He covered his face with his angocha and sobbed loudly.

No one would ever go to the Deputy Commissioner's home to make inquiries about a servant's death. The corpse-washer had soon prepared Taji for the final journey, and Khala Bi wept loudly after her last glimpse of the girl. Amma Bi stood quietly and stared. Malik had been told that Taji died of typhoid. He drank an entire bottle of liquor and lurched about trying to forget his sorrow.

'Who will ever make such parathas again,' he stammered. 'Taji's dead, now who will make such parathas . . .'

'Farewell, Taji,' whispered Sajidah. She kissed her brow and went to Taji's room.

The smell of blood pervaded her deserted quarters. The lantern in the alcove still flickered. She picked up Taji's filthy pillow and hugged it to her chest. She had yearned to weep for years, and now she finally burst out sobbing.

'Taji!' she wept. 'The day will come when rooms like yours are no longer filled with the stench of blood. It will, Taji, it will!'

She spoke with great faith as though Taji stood right in front of her, and with that same faith, she wiped her tears and smoothed out the pillow affectionately. As she was turning away from the bed, her eyes fell upon two tiny kameezes and four cloth diapers. Her heart once more filled with longing. She picked up the diapers and kameezes and pressed them to her bosom, then made her way to her own room.

Taji was already gone. There was stillness all around—not even the sound of scolding voices. Sajidah wrapped the kameezes and diapers in paper and placed them in a basket. She walked to Khala Bi's room and as she passed through the hallway she saw that Malik lay alone on the floor of his room. Everyone else's doors were closed. She wondered if they were all sitting alone in their rooms, mourning Taji. She walked outside silently. What was the gardener thinking as he sat resting his head on his knees? When she called out to him, he started.

'Call me a tonga, Mali. Did you not go to bid Taji farewell?'

'It wasn't the Mistress's order, Sajidah Bibi.'

He stood up and walked out of the gate. Sajidah wondered how he could have dared to speak up. Was his own life not dear to him, Khala Bi?

She stood and gazed at the verdant lawn for a few moments. That tree where she had seen Taji and Kazim's shadows on moonlit nights looked hopelessly rotted.

When she got home, Nazim was playing with Asad and Ahmed. He looked extremely happy, but when he saw Sajidah, all the blood drained from his face.

'What happened, Sajidah, did . . .?' he grabbed hold of her shoulders.

'Taji's dead, Nazim!'

'What? How did she die?' he asked tearfully.

Sajidah removed the tiny kameezes and diapers from the basket and spread them out on the bed. She picked up Asad and held him tight.

'Taji died so quietly, she didn't even say anything—at least not to Kazim . . .'

'She was in love with your brother at first,' said Sajidah, cutting him off. 'And by the time she wanted to flee that wretch, he had become the Deputy Commissioner, do you understand?'

Sajidah put Asad down and began to fold up the clothing hand-sewn by Taji. She felt overwhelmed. The hatred in her eyes shocked Nazim.

'I may be Kazim's brother, but I am not him,' he said.

Sajidah suddenly came to her senses. She looked at Nazim with embarrassment, picked up the clothes, and put them away in the trunk. Nazim began to gather up his writing things.

The night was so still and desolate that even the children's soft breathing sounded like mourning. Sajidah and Nazim ate a few bites and then lay down quietly. She wondered where Nazim's friends had disappeared to. If only someone would come tonight, there'd be some activity; then perhaps Nazim would be distracted. Today, for the first time, she had shown him her heart. What must he be thinking?

'Nazim,' Sajidah called out to him softly.

'Listen, Sajjo, I refuse to recognize Kazim as my brother.'

Just then, there was a loud knock on the door. Sajidah stood up quickly.

'Don't get up,' she said. 'I'll go see who it is.'

Lali came rushing in the moment she opened the door. She was sobbing, her face red as coals. Sajidah realized that Lali had been whipped by her husband again. She hugged her and brought her into the room. When Nazim got up to leave, Lali cried out, 'Don't go, Nazim, my brother, I've come to live here now!'

Nazim stopped in his tracks, astonished.

'Today, he beat me again; he cursed my father! So, I hit him back. Isn't that what you told me to do, Sajidah Baji? You said, "Hit him back!"' Lali continued, 'When I was leaving, he ran after me, but then he stopped. Now he'll kill me—I know how these landowner-types are, how they . . .'

She covered her face in her dupatta and began to sob.

For a moment, there was silence, then Sajidah looked at Nazim with fear in her eyes, but he gazed back proudly.

'He can't hurt you, Lali. If he kills you, then who will be the heir to his property? He's already left his sons,' she said to comfort Lali, but deep down inside she was terrified of what might happen. The minds of landowners are like salted earth, which cannot turn green even with abundant irrigation.

'Sister Lali, have you eaten dinner?' Nazim asked quietly.

'Dinner always begins with mention of the missing acres. All the same, I have eaten.' She'd stopped weeping and turned thoughtful.

'Don't you worry, Lali. Everything will be fine. Nothing ever stays suspended in the middle; it's always this way or that, right?' said Sajidah, lovingly tapping Lali's shoulder. 'You and I will sleep here, and Nazim will sleep in the sitting room, all right?'

Nazim had stood up and was about to go into the other room, when there was a light knock on the door. Lali jumped up violently, and Sajidah's heart sank. Nazim opened the door, and for a short while they could hear talking on the veranda. Then, Nazim entered the room with Zamindar Sahib. He was smiling.

'Let's see, Sister Sajidah. Lali hit me and then came over to you, so now please tell her to come home; the house feels deserted.'

Lali still had her arms around Sajidah. She stared sharply at Zamindar Sahib.

'Brother, she will not go!' cried Sajidah with determination.

'Please let go of your anger now—Nazim Sahib was angry, and now you are, despite being my sister. But try to understand, if we had those twenty acres, Lali's forthcoming son would be the region's greatest landowner. Her father cheated me, you know. But anyway, now I promise I'll never hit her again.'

'Go, Lali,' said Sajidah.

She grasped Lali's hand and pulled her up. Lali went and stood with the Zamindar as though there wasn't any problem at all. But yes, the marks of victory were clear on her face.

When the two of them had left, Sajidah thought for a long time. If only Taji had become Lali just once—and told the truth—she wouldn't have died like that, vilified and slandered.

35

The streets are empty
Where Mirza roams alone . . .

Nazim's friend Raza had commented on Sikander Mirza's government and everyone praised him as though he himself had locked Sikander Mirza up in Hujra Shah Muqeem. Another heated debate had begun, but Sajidah was bored of the conversation today. She was wondering what these people accomplished by expressing their views. They were just rehashing other people's words. Does anyone ever follow Lao Tzu's advice—that one must govern with the same love and care as one would use to cook small fish? When had their emperor ever followed this teaching? He had only followed Lao Tzu's directive—*leave my kingdom by all means but leave your knowledge and wits behind.* What need had an emperor for knowledge and wits? He had many other weapons and servants at his disposal to rule with.

Sajidah got up and went into the kitchen. Ever since morning, she'd been wondering how everyone fared at Malik's house. Much time had passed, but no one had come to visit, nor had they visited themselves. Taji's death had distanced even Nazim from that household. He never spoke of them any more. All they knew was that Kazim had been promoted. He was now the Commissioner. And then she began to wonder what would become of this country where bureaucracy ruled and the notion of democracy suffered miserably. Anything could be stirred into a storm; anything could become the stuff of bribes. Suddenly, she felt angry. What had Nazim turned her into? Now, she no longer had the leisure to think of anything else. And where must Salahuddin be now? Her Sallu—where had he disappeared? Tears came to her eyes. She wiped them away and started the tea, placed the cups on the tray and went into the sitting room where she set the tray on the table. She stood there, looking around at everyone as though they were strangers.

'Do sit down, Bhabhi,' said Qasim.

'What will I accomplish by sitting?' she murmured. 'What will you people get out of sitting in rooms and chatting like this?' She stared at them all. 'Have some courage! Go out into the streets and lanes, give voice to the people, give them a sense of their deprivation. Even a mother doesn't sense a child's hunger if it doesn't cry, and . . .' She turned abruptly, leaving everyone astonished. She went into the other room and fell upon the bed. Perhaps, she'd done the wrong thing . . . perhaps . . . who knew what Nazim would think!

36

It was a holiday, so Sajidah left the children with Nazim and went to Malik's house. She got down from the tonga and hesitated when she saw the two gleaming new cars. A uniformed driver and an unfamiliar servant looked her over critically. Had the old gardener not come up and greeted her, she might have turned back.

'You're visiting after such a long time, Sajidah Bibi! You didn't even come for Kazim Miyan's wedding. The younger mistress has been ill for so long—she's very unwell—you didn't even come to see her.'

The gardener spoke as he walked with her to the house. She opened the door and entered the hallway. The décor was so changed she felt as though she had come to the wrong place. She could hear voices and laughter coming from the drawing room. She entered Khala Bi's room quietly, and found her lying drowsily as though she'd been given a sleeping draught. Had her face not been visible above the sheet, Sajidah would have mistaken her for an emaciated child.

'Khala Bi, Khala Bi,' Sajidah called out softly.

Khala Bi opened her eyes. 'Sajidah, Sajjo dear . . .!'

Tears streamed down her face, soaking the pillow.

'No one told me that you were so ill, Khala Bi!'

Sajidah held her weak hand and caressed it.

'Kazim got married. He didn't allow us to invite you. Your Amma Bi didn't take part in the wedding either. After Taji's death, she stopped coming outside. She stays holed up in her room all the time. I feel like a criminal now.' She spoke haltingly. 'Saleema didn't come either . . . she only comes home during the holidays. She sits beside me for a few minutes, then leaves, and Malik is always drunk. He's completely unaware of the world. If he comes to see me, he falls over. I can't lift him up any more, so he just lies there. There's no one here to pick him up.'

Tears rolled down her cheeks.

Sajidah's heart was breaking. Who was to blame and who blameless? She heard chuckling in the drawing room, and she wished she could go and claw everyone's faces. *Everyone is laughing, everyone is lost in their own little world, and this living corpse lies here alone, dozing, and Saleema . . .* And she wondered as an elderly woman might: *Do mothers give birth just to see this day? Is Saleema this heartless? Why is she not here? Why is she not here, at her mother's bedside?*

'Khala Bi, you'll be better very soon. How can this household run without you?'

'I'm very tired now, very tired.' Khala Bi sighed deeply.

'You can't ever be exhausted, Khala Bi! You . . .'

Sajidah was trying to draw on the wisdom of the psychology books she'd read. Khala Bi looked at her oddly and smiled.

'Go, go to Saleema's room. She comes home and hides away in her room.' Then something inspired her to add, 'Who knows if she's come home or not. Kazim and his bride both take good care of her, but no one can get her to talk to them. But yes, how are the children? How is Nazim?'

She dozed off without waiting for Sajidah's reply.

Sajidah got up and went to Saleema's room. She was surprised to see that she lay on her bed with her eyes closed as though sleeping. Her full round face had grown gaunt and her milky white complexion was sallow. She opened her eyes and shot Sajidah a sharp look.

'Oh, my, Sajidah Bibi! How did you slip in here today?'

'The same way you slipped in and no one had any idea whatsoever.'

'I've been coming here like this for a long time, Sajidah Bibi,' she said, sitting up.

'Saleema Baji, what has happened to you? Don't you know that Khala Bi's extremely ill? She longs for you, and here you are just showing your face to her and then disappearing. She's your mother . . . a mother . . .' Sajidah said tearfully.

Saleema flushed, and her eyes hardened. Suddenly, Sajidah found it difficult to look at her.

'Sajidah Bibi!' she said, her voice shaking, 'Have I ever asked you to account for your life? What gives you the right to come here today and make these accusations? How dare you demand an explanation from me!' She paused for a moment. 'If you really want to know, here it is . . . You know how there's always a father as well as a mother? Well, where's my father? He died, didn't he? Good thing too, or he'd have ended up consumed in the fire that's destroying Amma Bi, and me, and everything else.'

'Are you saying these things about your own mother, Saleema Baji?' she asked with alarm.

'No, Sajidah Bibi. No, I'm talking about the kind of woman that would turn a bride into a widow . . . and the poor thing doesn't even realize she's turned herself into a maidservant, into an ayah. She pushed her own daughter from her lap and replaced her with the sons of another, and do you know why? So that she could prove her love. I, too, am a woman, Sajidah Bibi! But I don't want to turn out like my mother. I cannot snatch someone else's love away; I cannot deprive anyone of their right to love. Hate is much better than a love like that.'

Sajidah started and stared at Saleema as she continued to blurt everything out in one breath.

'I know, Sajidah Bibi. Hatred is one of the heaviest burdens in the world. A person weighted down by it will be crushed. All the same, hatred reigns supreme over my life. I hate my mother, my own mother!'

Saleema stared at the ceiling as though trying to decipher a piece of writing.

'Sometimes I think, if only there were someone here like your father, someone who could at least keep the record straight. Everyone here is weight-cheating—no one belongs to anyone. It's a strange kind of selfishness. Everyone drags their heels as they walk in anguish towards their graves—but to each his own accounting! Only Kazim is unconcerned with any accounting, even that of Allah himself!'

Sajidah's head began to spin. She was struck by both anger and sympathy. She felt as though all words had been wiped from her consciousness. She tried to speak but found she could not. It was during this confusion that Saleema suddenly had a severe coughing fit. Her eyes bulged from her head and looked twice as large. She pulled a handkerchief out from under her pillow and clapped it over her mouth to muffle the sound, but her laboured breathing could not be disguised. She ran to the bathroom. There, too, she coughed violently. A little while later, Sajidah thought she heard sobbing. She opened the door and went inside. Fresh blood glistened in the washbasin and Saleema was calmly washing it down the drain.

'Saleema Baji! What is this?' She was terrified when she saw the blood.

'Nothing. Stupid nosebleed had to happen right now.'

Sajidah stepped forward and grasped her hand, only to discover that Saleema was burning hot.

'You have a fever, Saleema Baji. You're very ill, you must go to the doctor!'

'The doctor! Why? What's it to me? I'll get well on my own. You have small children and you must look after Nazim as well—the poor thing has sacrificed his health for the sake of his country. In the meantime, look at Kazim, he's becoming quite the fat cat.'

Saleema lay down on her bed and closed her eyes. The circles under her eyes looked darker. Sajidah stood silently watching her, till she began to feel claustrophobic. She needed fresh air. She tiptoed into the hallway and stood there as though she were waiting to be called into the dining room. She walked in without really noticing what she was doing. A carpet covered the floor from one end to the other. Velvet curtains hung in the windows that matched the bright colour of the carpet. A large, beautiful table gleamed in the centre of the room and around the table were arrayed painted chairs, decorated with pillows that also perfectly matched the carpet. Glass cabinets stood to one side, filled with china and silverware neatly arranged so it could easily be counted. Everything was new; not a single item was familiar. Even the colours of the walls had changed. She didn't have the courage to step across the threshold, so she stood there, thinking, *The whole house has become echoing and empty. It feels as though ghosts live here and this room is dressed up like a bride. The drawing room must be even more lovely, and Kazim and his bride's bedroom more spectacular than that.*

37

Sajidah could find no peace that night. At times, she saw Saleema's sallow face before her and then Khala Bi's skeletal form. Sometimes, she heard Malik calling out for water and at others, Kazim's guffaws. When she recalled what Saleema had said, she'd sit up in shock and wonder if the truth really was so bitter. If Saleema hadn't had that coughing fit, who knew what else she would have said. How long had that lava been boiling inside her? If Sajidah hadn't annoyed her, would the dam ever have broken? Would her tongue ever have been loosed? Who knows, perhaps Khala Bi had made all these sacrifices for Saleema's sake. How could a woman raise a little girl alone? How could she protect her daughter? Couldn't Khala Bi have married Malik if she had wanted? But she hadn't. Then why did tears come to her eyes when she mentioned Malik's helplessness? Why had she taken on the sin of concealing the lies behind Taji's death for Kazim's sake?

She was frightened by her own thoughts. She tried to brush them away but thoughts have their own strength, they can climb higher than the skies, or sink to the nadir of the earth. No one can stop their path. Sajidah's thoughts wandered through Malik's home. *What a big heart Amma Bi had*, she thought, *to silently tolerate everything, after knowing all. But why was I surprised by Saleema's words? I've seen much of this myself ever since I set foot in that house. Does the truth need to be spoken aloud? Was it necessary for Saleema Baji to explode in order to give me a sense of the relationships between the people living in the household? How strange we humans are! What sort of place is this, where a daughter begins to hate her mother and a wife her husband? Why is it that the one who has the greatest opportunity to commit crimes or loot or kill is the one who becomes the most eminent and respected? Why were we all born? Why can we not face reality and truth? We're so weak that we're frightened of people who are like us, we bow before them, we avoid looking them in the eye, we fear asking them for our rights!*

Questions continued to swirl in her mind, advancing like a swarm of locusts. She got out of bed and paced about barefoot.

Malik's home might well be the mansion of Commissioner Kazim now, but he too should shoulder some of the household's responsibility. He was at the root of the conflict. The family had broken up because of him. He neither cared for Amma Bi nor Nazim—which was fine—but Khala Bi and Saleema had some claim on him. He should be attempting to cure them, and he should hire an employee to look after Malik. She would go tomorrow evening and speak with Kazim. If he didn't like it, too bad. What did she care what he thought?

This gave her some peace, and she fell asleep as soon as she lay down.

38

Kazim had created an office in a room outside the house. He sat there in the evenings and met with petitioners. There was a small garden outside the office, and now this had been made elegant as well, with eleven or twelve chairs set out where visitors waited to be summoned. The chaprasi who called out the petitioners' names at Kazim's court stood guard at the doorway. He was Kazim's special employee, and everyone knew that he could deliver someone to Kazim Sahib's presence in just a few minutes if he wished.

As Sajidah walked by the office, she suddenly noticed a familiar face among the visitors. She stopped and looked intently, then whispered to herself, 'Sallu! Where are you?' She began to shake like a leaf. The man, along with a few other callers, turned to look at her, and then began to chat with someone sitting nearby.

No, my eyes have deceived me. This man fitted out in a shark skin sherwani couldn't possibly be Sallu. Sallu is thin and handsome. If he were Sallu, he would run over to me and I would forget everything and embrace him. This must be some other man, but how he does resemble Sallu!

When she turned to enter the house, muttering to herself, the gardener came up and greeted her. As she stopped to inquire after his health, the man who looked like Sallu got up and rushed over to her.

'My goodness, Sajidah! Is that you? What are you doing here?'

Sajidah wished she could run and throw her arms around his neck, weep to her heart's content, tell him her woes, and ask him where he had disappeared. She wanted to tell him how she had waited for him, how she'd not been able to forget him for even a moment. But this person had built a wall between them; he wasn't the least bit happy to see Sajidah before him. He was but a cipher, a dry well.

'Sajidah! How are you?' he asked. Suddenly embarrassed, he corrected his error. He should have asked that question first, but his tone remained dry.

How different he was from the Sallu whom Sajidah saw in her dreams every night; the one who promised in every dream that he would find her one day. She always had faith that those dreams were true, but Sallu had taken so many years to fulfil his promise. She looked at that face again that she'd longed to get just one glimpse of for so long, but there wasn't the faintest sign of love there.

She pulled herself together. Life had taught her that art.

'I'm fine, but how did you come to be here?' she replied softly.

'I've come to meet with the Commissioner Sahib, but what are you doing here?'

210 Khadija Mastur

'I . . .' Now her voice was steady as well. 'This is my father-in-law's home, and Kazim . . . he's my husband's younger brother.' She threw a pebble into the well, hoping there might be some water in its depths, that he might be saddened to hear that she belonged to someone else now. But his look of surprise was now mingled with admiration.

'Oh, so you're Commissioner Sahib's sister-in-law!'

His words cut through Sajidah's heart like a dagger.

'That really is wonderful, because I've travelled a great distance with a letter of recommendation to meet Commissioner Sahib, but, oh my, now I see it's all in the family.' His face was glowing. 'I have to get a mansion allotted to myself here, if Commissioner Sahib pleases; then I'll be able to accomplish what I need to,' he said, presenting his request before Sajidah. But she was staring at the delicate vine that covered the wall of the Commissioner's office with its tiny leaves.

'Where do you teach nowadays?' she asked, addressing herself to Sallu as though in a dream.

'I live in Sargodha.'

Perhaps he hadn't heard her entire sentence because he added, 'I own a lot of land there. I've got an orchard on fifty acres; really good malta in my orchard, pure blood-red. My wife also received one hundred twenty-five acres in her dowry, so that makes the two of us the biggest landowners in the region. All the officers come and stay with us.'

Sajidah was shocked to find that both Sallu's words and his manner of speaking had changed. As he enumerated the size and qualities of his land, his voice rose with pride and his chest expanded. And his list of accomplishments was not yet complete.

'My two sons study at Chiefs' College. Two jobs have been set aside for them when they graduate. All the same, one must keep going back and forth. Next time I come, I'll bring my wife to meet you as well.'

Sajidah hadn't had sufficient reprieve to scrape away any old memories from Sallu's heart. She couldn't even tell him that she didn't live in this bungalow. She was thinking of something to say to him when Chowdhry Salahuddin saw the Commissioner coming out of his office. He forgot Sajidah completely as he rushed over to Kazim, bowing and salaaming so low he could have touched his feet. Then he disappeared among the other petitioners who had encircled Kazim. Sajidah felt her heart pricked by thorns, as though a corpse in a shroud had passed by. She walked away from the house, terrified.

Near the gate, she heard an elderly voice: *My daughter! Where is my daughter?*

She looked around, full of horror, but there was no one there, only the rustling of the leaves. Her legs began to tremble, so she leaned against a wall, and then sat down to sob, the earth soaking her tears as they fell on its bosom.

On the way home, the tonga seemed to move more slowly than usual.

'Bhai, can't you drive a little faster?' she urged the driver.

He brandished the whip over the horse, and it began to race along, its shoes sending sparks over the pavement.

Who knows what Nazim must be doing right now? she wondered as she wiped the tears from her eyes.

Afterword

I. Historical Context

A Promised Land begins in 1947, with the creation of Pakistan, and continues until around 1954. The majority of the historical events mentioned in the book are related to Nazim's activities and conversations. Nazim, the elder of the two brothers in the household, is a leftist, and had been an activist for the creation of Pakistan before Independence. In the new nation, he quickly transforms into a dissident as the new government and bureaucracy begin to work against the ideals espoused by proponents of its creation. Pakistan's founding father, Muhammad Ali Jinnah (often referred to as 'Quaid-e-Azam' or 'great leader') died on 11 September 1948, thirteen months after independence was declared on 14 August 1947. When Nazim announces his death to the family, everyone is shocked. It is a profound moment in the young nation's history, akin to Gandhi's assassination on 30 January 1948 (an event that is also referred to during a family quarrel).

In the beginning of the novel, Nazim works for the Department of Refugee Rehabilitation. It is under the auspices of this governmental organization that he visits the Walton Camp where Sajidah and her father are staying. During Partition, millions of people fled their homes on both sides of the border, sometimes in a matter of moments. Often, these were homes where families had lived for generations. The people who fled had no idea if they would ever return home—and often imagined they would—once things subsided. Usually, they would take just a few valuables, if they had time, fix a padlock on the outside door of their home, and join *kafila*s (processions of refugees fleeing on foot) or board trains, boats and airplanes. Many were killed in the process. Once refugees arrived in the new land, they were generally sheltered at government-run refugee camps, if they managed to find them.

Rehabilitation on both sides of the border involved finding homes and employment for the refugees; often, these were homes that had been abandoned by people who had recently fled the country. It was not uncommon for refugee families to take initiative and break the padlock on a house themselves and establish squatters' rights. But rehabilitation officers such as Nazim were specifically charged with matching people with abandoned housing that was in some way similar to what they had owned before Partition. Nazim asks Sajidah's father to fill out a form and have it witnessed, stating what assets he had left behind. This is the context in which her father, with Nazim's coaching, exaggerates his losses, and for the first time, fudges his accounts after a lifetime of honest bookkeeping, an offence for which Sajidah blames Nazim for many years. This system of note-taking and redistribution has been documented in many works of literature that take place in the aftermath of Partition, particularly in Bhisham Sahni's

Hindi novel *Tamas*. Krishna Sobti also alludes to the inflation of lost assets, and how refugees are disparaged for it, in *A Gujarat Here, A Gujarat There*.

Nazim later explains to his father that his reason for leaving this job was the widespread corruption at the agency, something his own family has actively participated in. In scene after scene, Malik regrets the loss of a mansion and orchard that his sons have never heard of, and that Kazim, as an enthusiastic proponent of bureaucratic corruption, embraces and seeks to have remedied through refugee allotments. Over time, Sajidah also learns that in pre-Partition India Nazim's family lived in three-room government quarters, but managed to break the lock on their mansion in Lahore and lay claim to an abandoned Hindu home. The paintings in the alcoves of Sajidah's bedroom indicate that the previous occupants had kept their Hindu idols there.

Mastur does not dwell on historical moments, but is able to capture political currents with deft strokes to indicate the passage of time and the divergence in the paths of the brothers, Nazim and Kazim, with the former following the path of a leftist dissident, and the latter of a corrupt high-ranking government bureaucrat. For example, when Nazim is jailed and tortured for many months for his involvement in political activities that are not described in any detail, we know that we are about four years after the beginning of the novel. The details of his arrest correspond to the crackdown on leftists in retaliation for the Rawalpindi Conspiracy, a failed coup attempt to overthrow the elected government of Prime Minister Liaquat Ali Khan. He is, in fact, in jail when Liaquat Ali Khan is assassinated, an event which occurred in 1951. The Qadiani riots (also known as the Lahore riots) that occur later in the book refer to the 1953 riots against the minority Ahmadiyya Muslim community, a time when martial law was imposed in Lahore by the Pakistan Army.

II. *A Promised Land* and Partition Literature

Partition has been a continuous focus of literary attention in the subcontinent since it occurred in 1947. Like the Holocaust, or the American Civil War, or the French Revolution, or any other epochal historical conflict that has shredded the fabric of society and caused many deaths, it is both a deep psychic preoccupation and an attractive literary device. When the mould of culture and society is broken, everyone and everything must be reconstituted. New patterns, customs and norms develop. Unspeakable violence, trauma, loss and nostalgia are hallmarks of the most well-known Partition narratives, such as the Urdu short stories of Sa'adat Hasan Manto, Bhisham Sahni's Hindi novel, *Tamas*, and in English, *Train to Pakistan* (Khushwant Singh), *Midnight's Children* (Salman Rushdie) and *The Shadow Lines* (Amitav Ghosh).

Perhaps the reader has noticed that all of these writers are men. This is because women writing about Partition have generally approached the event quite differently. It would be tempting to make a male-outside/female-inside comparison. Women's writing around the world has had a tendency to focus on interiority and literal interiors; the outside world, and the sweep of history, have belonged to men. But consider Qurratulain Hyder's Urdu novel *Aag ka Dariya* (River of Fire), for example, which provides a vast narrative spanning thousands of years of Indian history. Hyder does not focus on violence against women, or personal trauma (her characters are not in Punjab or Bengal, where most of the violence occurred, but many still end up migrating to Pakistan), but on civilizational violence, loss and trauma. In *Aag ka Dariya*, Partition and colonialism destroy a cultural ecosystem and set off a diaspora of wanderers and lost souls (in this category, she includes the British who had lived in India).

Altaf Fatima, in her searing Urdu novel *Dastak na Do* (Do Not Knock, 1963), set in the countryside near Lucknow, depicts an idyllic but deeply flawed society abruptly dislodged and stripped of assets that reconstitutes itself in an equally flawed manner in Pakistan. Watching her mother experience the trauma of displacement, the main character, Gaithi, abandons her own seemingly indomitable spirit and slowly evolves into the sort of woman she never wanted to be—one just like her mother. To Fatima's jaundiced eye, the extreme changes wrought by Partition somehow managed to fix nothing.

Khadija Mastur's two novels, *A Promised Land* and *The Women's Courtyard*, both deal with Partition. In the first, *The Women's Courtyard* (1962), the novel ends shortly after Partition, and despite the heroine Aliya's sadness, the changes brought about by her immigration to Pakistan have helped her break out of the confining space of the titular inner courtyard and allowed her access to the outside world. *A Promised Land* begins with Partition and was written some twenty years after *The Women's Courtyard*. By now, the shine has worn off of the promise of Pakistan for Mastur, a ferociously dedicated progressivist writer. The new land has not proven egalitarian as promised, and the conditions for women have shown no improvement. Greed for land, corrupt bureaucracy and entrenched feudalism have all conspired to throttle democracy in its infancy, and Mastur draws a clear parallel between these social realities and widespread misogyny. Mastur makes it clear from the outset that she is perfectly aware of the violence against women that occurred during the Partition period, but in *A Promised Land*, she asks us to remember that misogyny and rape already existed and continued to exist without the help of historic upheaval and displacement.

III. Abduction, Feudalism and Partition

As many as 100,000 women were raped or abducted during the violence that occurred leading up to the Partition and following the drawing of the borders. The worst incidents of violence are said to have occurred in Punjab, on both sides of the border, but were also scattered across all areas with heavily integrated populations of Hindus, Muslims and Sikhs. Mastur alludes to this violence through the character of the old man in the camp who has lost his daughter. Sajidah is also painfully aware of what she has avoided, and shudders to think of a fate that could have been hers. But as with *The Women's Courtyard*, Mastur is less concerned with inter-community violence towards women than intra-community misogyny and violence.

In *A Promised Land*, a question of central importance to Mastur is why one should dwell upon the abduction and rape of 'our' women by 'their' men, when our men rape and abduct our women on a routine basis? In her pursuit of this question,

Mastur is ruthless and unstinting towards societal norms and traditions. Both the protagonist, Sajidah, and the household servant, Taji, are abducted from the refugee camp by members of Nazim's and Kazim's family and held against their will in their mansion. These are not the sort of abductions that are discussed in terms of Partition violence because everyone involved is a Muslim refugee from India; not only Sajidah and Taji, but also the members of the family that have taken them from the camps. But they are abductions nonetheless, and Mastur makes it crystal clear that both women were lured from the camp to the family's mansion under false pretences, and thereafter, held against their will. Sajidah eventually 'decides' to stay, but this is only because her options are perilously limited. There is no place in the new society for a single woman and she resolves to accept where she's ended up and demand what respect and power she can.

For Mastur, the abduction of women and the seizure of property and land are closely allied concepts. The upheaval of Partition left many women abandoned, as well as many pieces of property. Just as the unattended property must be reallotted, so too must the women. The corollary to this idea is that the men who possess the most property and land have the greatest authority over the unclaimed women. This is an ancient tenet of feudalism and we see it play out both with the regular beatings Zamindar Sahib administers to his wife Lali because she did not come with the promised land of her dowry, and with Kazim's increasing brazenness towards Taji, and then Sajidah, as his status climbs from student to Deputy Commissioner.

Taji, an uneducated woman abducted from the camp, is installed as a servant in the household, though she is no better than a slave. She is paid in food and lodging for her housework, and half-smoked cigarettes for her sex work. Could she have left the household? She repeatedly tells Sajidah not to tell anyone about her complaints or they will kill her, and she may have been right. But of course, they do kill her in the end, through repeated abortions and continuous sexual abuse. Sajidah is spared Taji's fate because she is educated, and she also enjoys protected status thanks to Saleema and Nazim. But when Kazim receives notice that he will become Deputy Commissioner, all bets are off. By virtue of his powerful new position, and the relative weakness of his father and brother, he is now considered the master of the house. He now feels he deserves an upgrade in terms of his rights over the women in the household, and it is on the very night that he learns he will be made Deputy Commissioner that he attempts to rape Sajidah. For Kazim, Sajidah is a step up from Taji, a fitting reward for his promotion.

Sajidah is then left with a stark binary choice between becoming Kazim's mistress or marrying Nazim and leaving the house. The choice of remaining a single woman within the household is no longer available to her. After failing to find Salahuddin, she chooses Nazim unequivocally (despite her lingering hatred for him), and re-enters the house as a daughter-in-law. She is no longer an unclaimed piece of territory, and is off-limits to Kazim as his sister-in-law. In the end, Mastur suggests, a traditional arranged marriage is not so different from an abduction. A bride is suddenly removed from her natal home without much leeway for consent, and placed in the home of a strange man whom she must get used to. Sajidah at least knows Nazim by now, even if she dislikes him.

III. Nazim's Sins

During the opening chapters of the novel, Nazim commits three unforgiveable sins in Sajidah's eyes. The first is at the Walton Camp, when he jests to the elderly man about his sorrow over his daughter's abduction. In Sajidah's first encounter with Nazim, he approaches the old man right when she was hoping to comfort him, and says:

> 'Baba! Who is this daughter you cry for? That was no daughter, Baba! That was the most valuable of looted goods. Your screaming won't bring her back. Your voice cannot reach her.'

He goes on to explain his remark as a commentary on the cycles of revenge between the Hindu and Muslim communities, but his explanation is lost on the old man, and Sajidah finds it crude and insensitive. Nazim's second offense is to coax her father into exaggerating his losses in order to collect the maximum possible rehabilitation allotments. It is regarding this that she confronts Nazim on the night he asks her to marry him, accusing him of pushing her father to make the first accounting error in his life. Nazim's explanation is that he was trying to help her father, and that that is how the game is played. Nazim's third and perhaps most egregious sin is to abduct Sajidah from the camp at her moment of most intense vulnerability and grief, using his cousin Saleema as a lure. This, Nazim explains, he did to protect her and her intelligence, and to keep it from dying.

From a certain perspective, Nazim is a great guy. Mastur depicts him as a decent, intelligent leftist intellectual, who does not rape women and stands up for his beliefs. At the same time, she does not allow us to forget his three sins, and Sajidah does not forgive him for these until the very end of the book. It is likely that he committed all three sins because he was already in love with Sajidah, or at least attracted to her. Under the conventional rules of romance novels, all three of these offenses would be considered charming manifestations of male affection. His reticence towards Sajidah within the house and his gentlemanly restraint (he never lays a hand on her until his brother does) would be considered exemplary, and when he tells Sajidah he loves her, the readers' hearts would melt, as would Sajidah's. And we would forget the things he did, writing them off as romantic foolery. But Mastur is not writing a romance novel; Sajidah refuses to forgive and forget, and Mastur will not let us do so either.

In fact, Sajidah continues to hate Nazim for many years into their marriage. In a powerful moment just after Taji's death, Sajidah lets fall the mask of marital normalcy to reveal to Nazim her still-festering hatred, shocking even herself:

Sajidah put Asad down and began to fold up the clothing hand-sewn by Taji. She felt overwhelmed. The hatred in her eyes shocked Nazim.

'I may be Kazim's brother, but I am not him,' he said.

Sajidah suddenly came to her senses. She looked at Nazim with embarrassment, picked up the clothes, and put them away in the trunk. Nazim began to gather up his writing things.

Sajidah hates Nazim because of the traits he exhibited when she first met him. These betrayed misogyny and moral turpitude, as well as depriving her of her own autonomy. A reasonable list of offenses. But there is also another reason why Sajidah does not see the romance of Nazim's behaviour towards her. This is because she is already living in a romance story in her imagination.

She has been in love with her childhood sweetheart Salahuddin for years. Salahuddin is from Sargodha, a part of Punjab that went to Pakistan, but she met him when he was going to school in Delhi. They had promised to reunite on the other side of the border. Sajidah's memories of her beloved Sallu haunt her dreams and sustain her imagination throughout her time after Partition. It is only when Sallu fails to answer Nazim's advertisement seeking information about him that she gives up on her dream of being rescued by her beloved and agrees to marry Nazim— whose willingness to post the advertisement is yet another example of his decency.

In the novel's surprising denouement, Sajidah encounters Sallu at last, in the garden of the family's mansion, awaiting Kazim in a throng of supplicants. To her horror, she finds her romantic hero to be the epitome of everything she has come to loathe: he is a greedy, pompous zamindar, kowtowing to Kazim to get an extra mansion allotted just for when he visits his sons who are in college in Lahore. There are no traces of his former love for her, and his only interest in her lies in the hope that she can speed up his corrupt request from her brother-in-law. Interestingly, though she holds Nazim's first words to her against him, she has failed to recognize the deep roots of Sallu's feudalist tendencies in his own first words, when he told her long ago:

> 'We've come from a village, we have land there, and many trees—mango trees—when they blossom, the cuckoos sing, and when they eat the unripe fruit, I kill them with my slingshot.'
>
> 'How can you kill them?' she asked, alarmed.
>
> 'Ha! Killing isn't all that hard. It's just a cuckoo; people kill other people too.'

Orchards are a critical unit of graft in *A Promised Land*. For feudal landownership, they are the *ne plus ultra* of assets: a lucrative crop that must be protected even from songbirds. It is only when Sajidah is confronted with the blatant land-greed of a mature Salahuddin that she truly becomes resigned to her marriage, and perhaps willing to love her own husband, whose values she has come to respect.

IV. The Enigma of Saleema

Though Mastur often writes about her characters' emotions and experiences with startling clarity and detail, she does not shy away from ambiguity. In *The Women's Courtyard*, Aliya's emotional landscape contains many recesses that remain closed off from the reader. While Aliya is a character of enigmatic depth and ambivalence, Sajidah's emotions are presented with much less ambiguity. Instead, it is the character of Saleema in *A Promised Land* that remains shrouded in deepening mystery throughout the book.

After many re-readings I continue to ask myself what makes Saleema tick. What is her secret shame? What doesn't she reveal to Sajidah or anyone else? Why does she shut down emotionally after Nazim and Sajidah marry, an event she herself strives to bring about? What makes her believe that a romantic or physical relationship with a man is not available to her? Why does she lie dying quietly at the end of the book, without informing anyone of her condition? What else might she have told Sajidah if she hadn't begun to cough up blood? Is she in love with Nazim? Or Sajidah? Does she harbour a horrible secret?

Saleema explains to Sajidah that her hatred for her mother stems from her mother's role in the joint family. A cousin of Nazim and Kazim's mother (Amma Bi), Khala Bi moved into Malik's household with her young daughter after her husband died. Malik was in love with her, and thus Khala Bi 'stole' his love from Amma Bi, in Saleema's (and Amma Bi's) eyes. What is not clear is the nature of Khala Bi's relationship with Malik. As Sajidah points out, Khala Bi could have married Malik and lived in the household as a second wife. For some reason she chose not to, and instead became a glorified maid or ayah. Saleema's aversion to love appears to stem from this dynamic. But she also clearly states that she cannot embark on an intimate relationship with a man, and that such relationships are entirely based on 'hunger'. These allusions suggest something murkier than an unrequited love for Nazim, perhaps some sort of earlier assault by Kazim, about whom she tells Sajidah, 'You have no idea how much pain he's caused me.'

It should be remembered that in a traditional household, a match between Saleema and one of her two male cousins would have been considered appropriate and even desirable. But Malik's household is not entirely traditional, and with the move to Pakistan and their newfound status and wealth, the traditional family structure is breaking up. No one seems to broach the idea of a match between Saleema and one of her cousins, but that doesn't mean that Kazim may not have taken advantage of proximity and tradition to impinge upon Saleema's physical autonomy. Taji only came into the household after Partition. When did Kazim's habit of sexual harassment and assault begin?

While Sajidah, Taji and Lali present a neat line-up of three scenarios for women seeking some degree of autonomy within patriarchal relationships with men, Saleema is the only character who turns her back on such relationships. Ultimately, this includes even friendships, as she no longer communicates with her favourite male cousin, Nazim. Instead, in her new life, she teaches at her college, lives most of the time in the hostel, keeps company with other women teachers and focuses on recreational activities such as singing and badminton. Her affect is flat and unemotional and she has put intimacy behind her. Sajidah is insulted by Saleema's behaviour and now that she is also a mother, she begins to identify with Khala Bi, provoking annoyance in Saleema by saying things like:

'Saleema Baji, what has happened to you? Don't you know that Khala Bi's extremely ill? She longs for you, and here you are just showing your face to her and then disappearing. She's your mother . . . a mother . . .'

By now Sajidah has assumed a traditional role within the patriarchal system and started to prioritize an idealized maternal instinct over Saleema's filial rage. Saleema's anger, her independence, her attitude towards love and romance, all give her character a startlingly contemporary resonance.

Saleema, like Aliya, is an attempt by Mastur to imagine a path forward in society for single women. Yes, she draws the curtain on each of these characters as they lie across their beds, crying tears of rage and frustration (and coughing up blood, in Saleema's case), but this, I suspect, is her way of leaving the way open for future women to break free from female dependence on hetero-normative coupling within a patriarchal society. Mastur demands a radical future for women, even if she can't envision the contours of the path.

Daisy Rockwell

Further Reading: Partition Literature in Translation

Altaf Fatima, *The One Did Would Not Ask* (*Dastak na Do*) (Heinemann, Oxford, 1993). Translated from Urdu and introduced by Rukhsana Ahmad.

Bhisham Sahni, *Tamas* (Penguin Books India, Delhi, 2016). Introduced and translated from Hindi by Daisy Rockwell.

Khadija Mastur, *Cool, Sweet Water* (Kali for Women, Delhi, 1999). Introduced and translated from Urdu by Tahira Naqvi.

Khadija Mastur, *The Women's Courtyard* (Penguin Books India, Delhi, 2018. Introduced and translated from Urdu by Daisy Rockwell.

Krishna Sobti, *A Gujarat Here, a Gujarat There* (Penguin Books India, Delhi, 2019). Introduced and translated from Hindi by Daisy Rockwell.

Qurratulain Hyder, *River of Fire* (Kali for Women, Delhi, 1998). Translated from Urdu by the author.

Sa'adat Hasan Manto, *My Name Is Radha: The Essential Manto* (Penguin Books India, Delhi, 2015). Introduced and translated from Urdu by Muhammad Umar Memon.

Acknowledgements

I am grateful to my editor, Ambar Sahil Chatterjee, for believing in this project, and to my copyeditor, Trisha Bora, for her meticulous work.

Many thanks as always to Aftab Ahmad for helping me through the more difficult passages; Manan Ahmed Asif for help on historical points; and Asif Aslam Farrukhi and Aamer Hussain for their support of my Khadija Mastur translations.

I am grateful to Naveed Tahir for her valuable help and contributions, and to the makers of the *Aangan* miniseries, who have coincidentally inspired so much fresh interest in Mastur's writing.

I am indebted to my husband and daughter for their ongoing tolerance of my translation habit, and to my cats, who have played an invaluable role in the production of this work.

Finally, this translation is dedicated to Salman Hussain, most dedicated of readers, in gratitude.